In Sasha Hom's *Sidework*, the narrator—a homeless Korean American adoptee—is fearless and funny, surviving with her family under the grind of capitalism and extreme financial precarity. She navigates the vicissitudes at a cafe shift, with much humor and grace, in prose that's by turns lyrical and gritty. A stunning novella.
—Vanessa Hua, *Forbidden City*

Sidework is a gorgeous and wrenching ode to the work we do out of necessity and the work we do out of love. Over the course of a single shift in a California diner, a homeless mother of four navigates a motley crew of co-workers and customers and one very haunted supply room. With razor-sharp wit the narrator recounts the loss of her family's off-grid life in an intentional community and their search for a new home. Sasha Hom is an extraordinary chronicler of motherhood, work, grief, and what it means to live an ethical life. I loved this stunning, harrowing, and hilarious novella.
—Laura van den Berg, author of *State of Paradise*

Sidework is named for all of the work that holds your restaurant experience together, which you only really notice if it isn't done. Hom's novella is funny, it made me hungry for food, people, conversation—and it made me realize how much of contemporary American life isn't described by so much of our fiction. A tender and compelling lyric examination of a life lived at the edges of other people's happiness, Hom's philosopher mother is just trying to make her

life work out—and do her sidework. *Sidework* left me feeling more human rather than less.
—Alexander Chee, author of *How to Write an Autobiographical Novel*

Like a single drop of water on a leaf, Sasha Hom's *Sidework* holds the whole trembling world inside one morning's breakfast shift. Its unforgettable narrator is a mother of four living between the land and a supercenter parking lot, hustling for tips in one of America's richest counties. Her perspective peels back an intimate, life-or-death relationship with the fire-scarred Northern California forest, but like her, you'll find yourself more wary of the customers who believe they can order well-being off of a menu. *Sidework* is electric with subversive humor and the anxieties of motherhood and climate change—and Sasha Hom is a radical, rooted, thrilling new voice in literature.
—Sarah Cypher, author of *The Skin and Its Girl*

SIDEWORK

www.blacklawrence.com

Executive Editor: Diane Goettel
Book Design: David Provolo
Cover Design: Zoe Norvell
Cover Art: "untitled" by Eduardo Jaime

Published 2025 by Black Lawrence Press. Printed in the United States.

SIDEWORK

Sasha Hom

To:
Dylan, Naima, Sora, Tuli, and Ahn.
You are my heart, my light, and my inspiration.

"i'm not a mother, but i know what it is
to nurse a thing you want to kill

but can't. you learn to love it. yes.
i love my sweet virus. it is my proof

of life, my toxic angel, wasted utopia
what makes my blood my blood."

—Danez Smith, *Homie*

SIDEWORK

all sidework must be done to keep things
running smooth—your mgr.

- Take out butter (first)
- Turn on lights
- Turn on heat
- Set up outdoor tables - put out condiment
  caddies, chairs, silverware buckets
- Start coffee (at 12-min b/f 7 only!)
- Fill all creamers
- Fill Sani-buckets
- Put ketchups on tables
- Fill salt (can be done at the end of the day)
  (if slow)
- Silverware buckets on <u>all</u> tables!
- Turn on **acceptable** morning music

Open/Close

January 5th, 2020, 6:30 AM

In the winter, when I open, there is no sunrise. At least, not yet. I have to remember to turn on the porch light. As my old manager said to me one slow morning, "No wonder there isn't anyone in here. They can't even see the front door!" Until the night lifts its skirt to reveal a strip—kind of pinky, like medium rare.

Sometimes I like to imagine that I'm inside of a snow globe, silver glitter raining on my hair, a homeless Korean American adoptee in braids—an Ajumah, really, but that's not how I like to think of myself—standing on the restaurant's front porch that creaks and crackles beneath my clogs feels like walking across an old ship's deck. Where just the other day my boss—the husband, noticed a board, a one by one, dangling from above, threatening to impale the next customer who tried to Come Again.

There are some days when I want to chuck this snow globe of a restaurant down the non-ADA-compliant walkway, past the Italian flowering tree that smells like grappa in the sunshine, over the coastal range, and straight to the bottom of the sea, where it will lull with the currents. Until some octopus suctions it up, pulling me into the whirlpool of its day. But I don't.

At this hour, people think it's so dark out here. But it's

6 o'clock, folks. There's light everywhere! Morning breath sparkles in the astronomical dawn, coating the wooden sidewalk with electric leaves. Dog owners walk their companions, back and forth, beneath mist passing through the wake of sodium lamps. They shine flashlights to illuminate the small thin line that they pace, cajoling, *Go potty now. Come on. Go pee pee.* While I flip chairs off of porch tables, in the shadows, waiting for the sun.

As the restaurant gurgles awake, I stand behind the swinging door, staring out the small round window into the street, praying, "Please, God, let this be a busy day. Please?"

Meep, Meep!

6:35 AM

At first, it's just me and the cook. He unlocks the back door with the key hidden behind the commercial ice maker. The Christmas lights strung year-round in the dining room pull us through the unlit hall. I switch on the overhead. He clocks in. I clock in, and then we say our good mornings.

In the kitchen, he lights the overhead grill that smells faintly of propane. I fill the red Sani-buckets. He takes out the bread. I pull out the butter from the mini fridge in our station and place it beneath the heat lamp to thaw. Wearing powder-blue latex gloves, he mixes potatoes with spices in a plastic gray tub. I line up small bottles to be filled. He asks me if I have a friend for him, one from my country.

I say, "Yes. In fact, I do. She looks a little like Margaret Cho. You like big women, right, Salvador? And, sure, she wants to have an affair with a married Mexican who works a hundred hours a week to pay his mortgage."

He makes a strangled sound.

"Mocha bianca?" I ask.

He nods and we both look up at the cameras.

"Extra shot?"

He pleads, "Yes. And not too sweet."

Then, together, we figure out the specials and get on our merry way.

It's a little like Wile E. Coyote and the sheepdog before they begin their shenanigans, barking at each other, tossing burnt toast through the window. And me—begging for favors and forgiveness the whole long day.

Refolded

6:45 AM

A couple walks into the restaurant before we've officially opened. They pause, momentarily, at the threshold, then proceed—she, in an oversized sweater; he, in a T-shirt—and seat themselves in the Backroom, in the coldest spot in the house. The Back 6. Or, "The Tom Waits," as we sometimes call it. Because it's where Tom sits. I weave through the off-set aisles to get to them. The way this restaurant is set up... "Labyrinthian," is what I tell my customers, unsure if that's actually a word.

The couple leans across their two-top, foreheads practically touching, talking intensely in hushed voices. The salt shaker on their table is half empty, or half full, depending on how you want to look at it. Whose sidework is salt today? God, I hope it isn't mine.

"Good morning," I say cheerily.

No response.

"Hi. Hey. How you guys doing? What can I get for you? Can I start you on anything to drink?" Sometimes I try all of the greetings, like a doorbell. But they don't even look up.

It's already been one of those days where when I wake, my son wakes too. My husband has to carry the crying baby away from the van where the other children cuddle for warmth like spoons in a drawer. I have to nurse in the parking lot, standing—the Walmart sign brighter than the sun, my bunched uniform baring a pale strip of my stretched-out skin—until he quiets and I can unlatch myself and drive the other old vehicle to work: the I-mark.

"Coffee?" I try again, but no one leans back against the wooden backs of their wobbly chairs to look at me. In fact, they lean in, as if I am just a ghost.

I'll talk to Raul about it, Love. Don't worry.

You really should've mentioned it to me last night.

I did, Love, when we were in bed.

Well, there you go. What do you expect? I was sleeping.

The upstairs of this restaurant is filled with ghosts. That's why no one likes to restock the To-Gos, the sugars, the napkins, or the salt. Especially the salt. But, as the memo behind the computer consul reads, **SERVERS!** Do **ALL** of your SIDEWORK. That means **EVERYTHING!**

"How about a drink menu?" I say.

The woman startles as if she's just seen an apparition with two menus tucked under its armpit. Crusted sleep clings to her lashes; one eye wanders. I always try to look people in the eyes when I talk, to appear as if I'm giving them my full service. But what to do if one eye strays?

"Oh drats," I say, out loud, because I have just placed their tri-fold menus on the table the wrong way. They're supposed to be arranged with the name of the restaurant, followed by the picture and story of the guy who this place is named after, face-up, so he can stare into your soul as your stomach growls. I try to rearrange the pages but, "They're like maps. You can never fold them back the way they were," I say, neglecting to mention that nothing's ever the same after it's been refolded.

"We'll only need one," the man says, raising one finger to clarify.

I set his one menu down, correctly refolded, but still not the same. The front door swings open and shut. The percolator spurts out its final dribble. The barista with Lyme slips in and I shiver.

"Coffee?"

They nod.

"Cream?" I try for eye contact.

The woman looks down at their one menu.

"Great! I'll be right back with that."

I return to my station. Except, I've neglected to fill all the creamers, which I was supposed to do because it's on my sidework list. You have to focus real hard to fill up the little soy sauce bottles with half-and-half. It's tricky, because if you pour it in too fast or put in too much, it spurts out like a geyser and can even shoot into your eye.

I put a creamer down on their table. The man pushes the soy sauce bottle to the edge. The woman pulls it back.

"I want eggs sunny side up," he begins.

"Uh huh." I nod, looking him in the eyes as I pour.

"Potatoes. Crisp. Sourdough toast—dry, and coffee. Black."

Now I recognize him by his order—the winemaker who bought the old Harris ranch. No one thought it would sell. The barn had collapsed. The soils were depleted. But with the housing shortage after the fires and gentrification…Then

I notice there's a beetle on their table. It's fluorescent green with black dots, spinning psychedelically on its back, and it unmoors me.

If it were a cockroach, per se—no problem. I'd swipe it to the ground. That's what I do when they scamper out of the silverware buckets. But this is a beetle, a black and green beetle, like a ladybug gone wrong.

The word, "cucumber beetle" pops into my head. I used to find them at the intentional community where we lived before everything went to hell in a handbasket, as they say. I'd bring a baby to the farm and she'd crawl away between the rows, her four skinny limbs scissoring quickly, cloth-diapered butt raised like a kind of beetle. She ate cherry tomatoes by the fistfull, maybe even a few cucumber beetles as well. You're not supposed to let kids under the age of one—or is it eighteen months? I can't remember—eat tomatoes, or pineapples for that matter. Too much acid. Her face would break out into a red bumpy sunrise, a shiny, rising patina all over her chubby cheeks. Now what kind of mother does that make me?

"Shit," I hear myself say as a black river flows out of the winemaker's small white cup, washing away the beetle.

He jumps quickly to his feet, pulling folded napkins out of the silverware bucket, and dabs ferociously at his crotch with the whole wad.

"Here, let me get a dish rag," I say. He reaches for more napkins from another table's bucket.

Not wanting him to grab any more napkins, I run back to the counter where the dishrags sit in a red bucket of blue chemical water. My boss—the husband, chides us if we waste. "Use a dish rag! Don't waste butters! You have no idea how expensive they are!" He'll stand right beside the dish bins, inspecting each plate as we slip them in, the stacks of dirty dishes growing heavier in our arms, yelling, "I don't want to see any butters on those plates! Too many unused jams! And why are there so many clean napkins?! Save the butters! Less napkins!" And even once, "The next person who trashes a butter is fired!" You know those thumbnail-sized individually packaged ones wrapped in gold foil. The old manager had to explain to him that he can't actually do that. Although, the new manager would probably let him.

When I return with the warm soapy rag in my hand, the couple has moved to Backroom table number 2, another two-top, which I am grateful for. Since I opened, Back 2 is also my table. All these tables are mine for the first half hour. Then B-girl, or boy, comes in and I move to the right half of the restaurant. Then C-girl, or boy, and I move to tables 1, 2, 3, 4, 5, 8, 9, Back 1 and Back 4, Out 1 and Out 6, I think. I can't remember. And then D-person comes and I lose all Backroom tables, then E, and I lose table 3, some Out tables. Then, later, as we cut, it all happens again in reverse. D goes to B; E goes to A; C stays the same. Until, like Survivor, there's only one server standing and all the tables are theirs.

My children named a baby chicken "Survivor" when we lived at the intentional community. He was eaten by ravens the following day. But survives in the illuminated memories of their minds.

"Sorry about that," I say, leaving the soggy brown dish

rag on Back 6. "Now what was it you wanted?"

I scritch-scratch my pen across the pad to resurrect the ink. I haven't had my coffee yet. Can't rely too much on the memory. Like a sieve, I tell customers when I forget things, tapping my temple with a writing implement or utensil, wishing my co-workers would put the pens back in the caddies correctly: point down.

"Eggs, sunny, sourdough toast. Potatoes," the winemaker repeats.

"That's right. Crisp," I say, not telling him that the cooks don't do "crisp" on Sundays.

"And what about you, Love?" I try to establish eye contact but she's watching her fingers pluck at the now frayed edge of her menu.

"I'll have the same," she says.

"Eggs, sunny. Sourdough toast, dry?"

"Yes. But. I'd like my eggs scrambled. And do you have any gluten-free bread? With butter. Actually, can you bring me extra butter? And add bacon. Please."

I nod, even though, Now, Hon, your order is not The Same. It dawns on me that the beetle must have hitchhiked here on her sweater. Because I have seen the winemaker many times and never have I seen him with a beetle.

"Can you believe…" I say, topping them off. "In all these years… I have never poured coffee like that!" I right the pot just as the coffee reaches the brim. The winemaker grimaces, but the woman makes eye contact and laughs.

The Supercenter

6:59 AM

The children should be up by now. They will have walked, bleary-eyed, up the aisles of a chain store they'd never set foot in until the last fire. The windows of the van will be fogged over from their sleep, the big dogs curled awkwardly on the seats, partially dangling.

They will lay toilet seat covers across the toilet seats before they sit on them. At least, the older ones will. The younger ones will squat with their shoes on the seats, hovering over the bowl. The olders will have to hold onto the wrists of the youngers as they perch so that a foot doesn't accidentally slip into the bowl. I see that the sun has risen, rendering the slight rain almost imperceptible. I hope the baby went back to sleep. The shopping carts always rattle him awake. The fine mist is just visible beneath the parking lot lamps, falling away in a triangle of pixelated light. The baby can be folded and held beneath the thighs while he pees. We use elimination communication, which, my husband says, just means your house, if you have one, is the diaper. *Home is where the Honda is,* we used to say. Although now we have a 15-passenger Ford van.

My husband will have to run the defroster to clear the windows. I hope no one peed on the mattress. He will have to stand outside the bathroom while the girls go in. They will hold the baby while my husband takes his turn. What will they look at, standing outside the men's room, surrounded by aisles filled with possibilities taller than their father? We're not consumers unless we're forced to be. I hope they wash their hands.

Conditions

7:00 AM

Christmas lights blink on and off, minus a few dead bulbs. The barista with Lyme is hunched over his disposable coffee cup, bouncing on the balls of his feet. His breath comes out in shallow wisps of gray. The closing server must have forgotten to slide the slim switch on the thermostat to "auto" yesterday. Or is it "run"? I can never remember which one makes the heat come on. But obviously, it has yet to come on today.

"I hate slow mornings," he says. The To-Go cup, stamped and stocked by yesterday's barista, caves between the force of his hands.

"Why don't you use a mug?" I ask, glaring at his pile of unstamped cups cluttering my area.

He picks at a scab and looks up at me as if to say, *It's not your sidework. Why should you care?* I glare back as if to say, *Get your fucking sidework out of my station.* He skulks off, wiping already-clean surfaces just in case someone is watching.

The laughter of Rosanna, the prep cook, buries the voice of some young female singer/songwriter crooning on the radio in the kitchen. The cook laughs loudly. He is dancing.

The barista with Lyme slices into a day-old lemon poppy seed muffin and offers me half, stuffing the other half into his mouth. He chews, staring into space, red-eyed and red-faced.

"Oh man, I love that lady's giggle," he says, blushing. "It's so dreamy."

Rosanna is a woman who likes her hot cocoa sweet. She rode *canids* across borders with babies on her back just to make us the best biscuits ever. I believe she only has three kids. Although one of them, she says, is still in Mexico.

"God dammit! Why do I have to have salt today?" I say, looking at my sidework list.

"Who's B-girl? Is it Shelley?" the barista asks, looking at the clipboard.

"You mean, 'boy.'"

His shoulders droop. "I love that man, but sometimes he can be such a baby," he whines, swiping crumbs from his smooth hairless cheek.

Why do we always preface our complaints about our co-workers with, *I love them, but...*? I think the barista is a little homophobic, if one can be a "little" homophobic. I mean, you either are or you aren't, right? I love that barista, but...

Outside, a young blonde in a pickup, its bed filled past the brim with hay, gives it too much gas. Her hair streams out of her window as she cuts the corner too close. I try to steer her forward with my mind, imagining bits of hay flying past my still-youthful eyes.

The kitchen door swings open and then shut.

"Chocolate?" Rosanna asks, pronouncing it the Spanish way.

The barista dashes over to his station and begins steaming milk. Rosanna smacks her hands against her apron. A cloud of flour rises, sending her into a coughing fit. When it clears, she sniffs the air.

"Mmm. What smell?" she asks.

"My lotion," I say, pointing at the little silver disc sitting on the counter of the server's station.

"Smell good," she says, her voice rising on the "good," practically singing it.

She once told me she had to pay "coyotes" $2500 to come here. That was fourteen years ago. Now, it's like $8,000 and way more dangerous. She rubs a dollop of cream into her brown cracked hands, their fine lines caked in white.

"You can keep it," I say, pushing the tin into her palm. "Walmart has a gazillion of them."

The barista returns with her chocolate, just the way she likes it. The oven timer beeps and Rosanna disappears through the swinging door, leaving my lotion—coconut rose—on the counter.

"Your table's calling you," the barista says.

I peer around the corner into the Backroom where the winemaker's lady friend waves her arms like she's shooing bees.

"So, they are," I say. "I wonder what they could want from me this time."

Dangling

On the property where we used to live there was a platform, a small round disc, perched on the tippy-top of a lopped-off tree. Like the kind of trees you see beneath power lines that look like asparagus spears bitten off by chainsaws so that the electric lines wouldn't, hopefully, set them on fire. From up there, you could see everything: our ocean of woods swaying, prescient and whispering; our farm stitched into the hillside; their army of vineyards marching up with their chainsaws, encroaching, slowly, with time.

At least, that's how I imagined the view. I'd never actually been up there. To my mind, that platform was just balanced and, in a strong gust, it would spin like a plate on a stick. But of course, it wasn't balanced. It was bolted. It even had sides, delicate railings of twisted fir branches about waist-high.

They called it The Crow's Nest, and it frightened me.

"That's a lot of faith to put in a tiny piece of hardware," I said to my fellow intentional community members, who just looked at me as if I were questioning the foundation of their bylaws.

It must have been on a Monday night, a community-dinner night. There was a boy in The Crow's Nest. He had scaled the nailed-in chunks of wood that passed for a ladder and was leaning against the railing, laughing drunk on altitude. I was doing the mother thing, where you try to hold them up with your mind, hoping that it's enough. Which, luckily, that night, it was. Later, he would suicide in the tiny house that he built himself with its one window his mother had insisted upon for light.

I thought, "Thank God it's her boy up there and not my boy," as mine was not yet crawling.

My daughter clung to the rungs, whining to follow him up.

"Not tonight, honey," I said, gently removing her hands.

How to explain? I couldn't hold any more children aloft with my head. Besides, we were on dinner. We needed curry and lentils, and the bulk of the food hadn't arrived yet. So, I had her cut green onions with the garden scissors instead, while the boy drank the moon like moonshine, leaning forward, his arms spread wide as he howled, or sang, or something. I could hear him from inside the cob indoor/outdoor kitchen. Beneath the stretched-plastic roof, looking up, I could see him leaning farther out from The Crow's Nest, his arms fanned out around him like he was a masthead on a ship suspended above a roiling arboreal sea.

More community members arrived and sat beneath the branches. They rolled thin cigarettes. They plucked guitars. A banjo. A sweet voice. A harmonica, a woven song rising. The wind came and everything swayed. The goats ascended, baa'ing with some dogs and more children, some of them mine. The temperature dropped so that flannels no longer cut it—not without a layer of wool at least. Our breaths collectively mingled into one communal puff, evaporating into the night.

A cardboard box filled with dumpstered zucchini, sliced

bread, pastries, burst papayas, and Traditional Medicinals showed up. I slit tea bags into the pot in lieu of curry, stirring the lentils with a wooden spoon. I ran the edge of the metal spatula along the bottom of the cast iron pan. Fried rice peeled away crisp, thin as lace. I cleaved squash on a wonky table. Their halves rolled away, gaining a lopsided speed. The dogs dashed after. The boy rocked, hands raised above his head, reaching for that space where leaf and branch meet sky.

BOH & FOH, just like friends

7:04 AM

The front door swings open and then shut. It's the busser. He smiles at me with just his lips, dipping his head so his afro bobs, and does his Gumby-walk across the warped wood floor.

"That man ain't right," the barista says, scratching at his calf with a pen.

"Oh, I don't know. I think he's nice."

People often wonder about that busser. Maybe because he doesn't talk. If you ask him how he's doing, he just says, "Peaceful." He used to work at Goodwill, sorting donations. I asked him what the oddest donation he ever received was. "A bomb," he said, smashing his lips into a smile.

Now there are more employees here than customers. But I know that won't last. I know the customers will soon come streaming, clogging up the aisles.

The front door swings open and shut. It's just Jorge, the second cook. He flashes me the peace sign. I flash it back. He clocks in, then disappears into the gaping maw of the kitchen as Freddie Mercury blasts out through the steam.

Usually, the cooks enter through the back. The swinging door bifurcates Back of The House and Front of The House like a border. Jorge, however, will walk through any door. I don't believe it's a political act. He's not the sharpest tool in the shed. One egg short of a carton. Not nice, I know. But I'll spell the whole order out for him:

Veggie Omelet, no cheese, biscuit, no potatoes, sub spinach

Veggie Omelet, wheat toast dry

Veggie Omelet scrambled, No Tomatoes! Biscuit

Veggie scramble

And can you believe what I end up with? Two scrambled veggie omelets with cheese and biscuits. One veggie omelet not scrambled without cheese, wheat toast with butter. And no veggie scramble at all! It probably doesn't help that while he's inspecting the ticket I'll yell, "¡Apúrate cabrón!" so that the dishwasher laughs, the other cook laughs, and the prep cook asks what I said. Then he laughs too because they always laugh whenever I say anything in Spanish, especially if it's about Jorge.

These are the games that we play. But if anyone were to ask me who holds the power here, I'd say the BOH because they have the bacon. *Where's my side?! Give it to me! I see it right there. It's gonna get cold! I need it! Please? You're gonna fuck up my tip.* But only the literal bacon.

I'll say "muy feo" when he gives me French toast with powdered sugar that looks like mouse turds. I'll say, "pinche burro," when he gives the Benedict to my co-worker before he gives it to me. I'll say, "qué pasó?", to indicate that he's out to lunch when we are still on breakfast. And you know what he says? "I love you, baby. God loves you, baby." I'll shoot him a look to indicate there's no precedent for love here, and he'll reply, "Muy mean on the outside. But inside, I know—mucho amor."

Legacies/The Virus

7:10 AM

A pile of menus stacked on the counter, threaten to topple over. The barista with Lyme sanitizes menus one at a time, then shoves them into their holder, which he's not supposed to do. It frays the spines and the boss—the wife—says it's very expensive to replace them.

He spritzes, wipes, and raises a bacteria-free menu, shaking it at me.

"Did you know that this guy..." He stabs his thumb at the picture of the man with two first names who this restaurant is named after, featured on the front-page of the menu, if it's folded right. "This pato, this maricón..." It bothers me whenever the barista uses Spanish slang, like this gringo thinks he's down. But he's not. How could we be? "... used to own everything. He owned the entire town. Not just half of it, like these foolios." He gestures towards the cameras. "They only own half. You know that right? They own the hotel across the street, the yoga studio where their daughter teaches, plus the building it's in, that new ceramics store— which is really just an expensive knick-knack shop. It's the other Italian family that owns the liquor store, the restaurant that serves dinner, the wine tasting shop, and the fish tackle place. It'd be like a *Romeo and Juliet* if both families hadn't had all girls. Although they could turn out to be lesbians, and then it could be a queer Romeo and Juliet with all these defunct ATM machines splattered throughout the town. Our bosses own those too. You know that, right? That's why we're Cash Only."

"I thought Matt owned the ATMs."

"He did. Before the flood. But back when the railroad ran through here, this guy, this fresa on our menu, owned it all. He owned the railroad, the mountain, the trees he sold to build the city where all the tourists come from on the weekends to visit what's left of the Redwoods. You know that tiny patch on Fitzgerald, like a pimple on the face of a vineyard, yo." He spits into a napkin.

"The Old Grove? I send my customers there all the time."

He takes another sip of his coffee. I look hopefully at the door.

"People always think this restaurant is where the train station used to be. That's partly the owners' fault. That's how they advertise it. They should've just outright lied and called this place The Train Station. But this was the hotel. The real train ran through the alley by the other restaurant owned by the other family, the one that serves dinner. I worked there for a heartbeat, but the owner reminded me too much of my pops, yo. Anal. I told you how my pops was a pilot before he died of cancer. All those metal detectors and then those vaccinations that they make you..."

"Then where'd all the tracks go?"

"They ripped it out and dumped it all on Ray Ray's land."

"Really? By the day spa?"

"Yeah, but I think the spa owner paid MBob to remove

it and he dumped it illegally somewhere on the Hormel Chili dude's 800-acres. Probably on that spot where everyone dumps their mattresses?"

"Oh yeah. I know the spot."

"So anyways, this guy, this..."

"Go on."

"... even owned the town with all those demonic, twisted, narrow streets named after San Francisco streets. I fucking hate driving through that town, man. Half the time I'm driving through it backwards because someone's coming at me head-on and I got to put it in reverse, hoping that someone doesn't do me from behind. Well, that whole town used to be housing for the Chinese working on the railroad, living on Stockton, Grant, Broadway—like a fucking China-town in the woods. Aren't you Chinese?"

"Me? No. Why? Do I look it??"

His face turns strawberry-red. "I thought you said you were."

"I'm Korean. I was adopted. By Chinese. Chinese Americans."

"Oh, right. I'm Irish. Irish-German-Italian-English, a little Jewish and Native American. I did one of those tests. So, anyways, homie decides to let his workers buy the houses that they were already renting. But with one caveat: They could only own the house, not the land. He would always own the land."

"Like an intentional community! Or, at least, our old one."

"So, after the railroad was built, he set all those houses on fire. Can you imagine that? All those Chinese with no job, no wife, no house, no land!"

"Where did they all go?" I wonder. "Because no Chinese Americans live here now."

"Some died, some suicided, some just sank right into these hills. And then, just like that—poof!—they were gone."

Fruits of Our Laborers

7:15 AM

And I still don't have a second table. Sometimes it's like this in the morning, and I know that it will pick up. I know that everything will work out and I'll walk out with more money in my pocket than I came in with because that is the nature of these jobs. But time hurts when it's slow. Although, some might say, you get used to that when you don't have a home to return to. You get used to hanging out at some public place, watching the sky turn its blues.

The barista stamps cups, trying to get a leg up on his sidework. The cook fries bacon. A customer walks through the front door with a small dog tucked under his arm like a newspaper.

The customer asks, "What kind of dog is that?" pointing out the window at a big mutt lifting its haunch over our sandwich board placed inconveniently in the center of the sidewalk.

I say, "It looks to me like a Rhodesian Ridgeback, Great Dane mix, with possibly a little bit of Rottweiler." The dog turns to sniff its own urine, then trots away in a hurry.

"Yeah. Yeah. I can see that." He goes to the bar and orders a drink.

"You don't want a table?" I call after, but it's useless.

Why, just the other day, about a mile away from the

intentional community where we used to live, my children and I saw a random dog digging in the middle of a big dirt field. We were driving through the valley near the ex-intentional community, between scorched hills like bent backs holding up an endless sky. There were meadows dotted with Live Oaks still living and a few ancient Valley Oaks hunched over. But where the apple orchard once stood, there was only a field of bared dirt. No trees! Just miles of rebar stabbed equidistantly into soil, raked diligently into parallel lines by laborers inhaling the earth's tainted dust.

The children were irate. I was shifting through the turns in our golden '82 diesel Isuzu I-mark with no available parts anywhere in this nation. The car bounced dramatically every time we went over a pothole, which we had not realized were so plentiful until we lost our rear shocks, five little black heads bobbing in the window.

"Why would they make another vineyard?" a child whined.

"I bet it won't even be organic!"

"Maybe it'll be organic?" I tried.

"I thought they were restoring the creek for the salmon?"

"They're planting lavender along the vines. For the pollinators," I tried, again. Was it Lao Tzu who said (according to Stephen Mitchell) that hope is as hollow as fear?

"Ach. Glyphosates! They're poisoning us!"

"Us? You mean the world, Ding Dong."

"But the bees."

The road smoothed and they quieted, turning around in their seats to watch, silently, one dog digging in its new desert, until it became smaller than a piece of fruit.

A kid asked, "What kind of dog is that?"

I said, "I think it was some kind of terrier."

The Last Ten

We have two dogs. They are both wolf dogs, but more dog than wolf. So, "low content." Big-ish. Obstacles to obtaining a rental, perhaps? It's not like we haven't tried. We scour the ads every day. Craigslist, the classifieds, detaching detachable phone numbers off fliers attached to public cork boards. Usually, they only want dogs 20 pounds and under. Dig that?! 20 pounds? That's a feline! Maybe if we put the bitch on a diet, we could call her an "almost-small-dog." But diets are difficult. She has the means to self-feed. She shimmies out of her harness. I think she detaches her shoulder—a real Houdini of a dog.

When we were camped in the tipi in the leech field at MBob's, with the sheep next door and the grower who pumped classical music through his speakers for his plants, night and day—*like camping outside of a frickin' 7-Eleven*—the dog would vanish and reappear, harnessed and every-thing, with bits of wool between her teeth. Once, with a puff of a tail. We had to leave before the rains came anyway.

After the intentional community, we moved at least once a month. That is, if you don't count the nights on the side of the road. There was that property across from the bike trail with the chicken with the bad legs. The bitch ate her too, and then we were asked to leave. We haven't lived in a house with sheet rock since the oldest—child, not dog—was crawling.

They will eat a plastic bag—dog, not child, at least, not usually. The male will bust through sheet rock if he's separated from us by a wall. This county has a 0% vacancy rate. Since the fires, it's probably in the negatives. There aren't many rentals under $1600 that allow dogs, regardless of weight. According to *The Times*, the largest growing segment of the homeless population is the middle-aged, single, white female. They don't say anything about families of six with two dogs.

I know the big apartment complexes will advertise, "Dogs Allowed!" But they have all those bloodline requirements... *No pit bulls, pit mixes, shepherds, or malamutes...*The parking lot at Walmart is so crowded now...*No fighting breeds, northern or hunting breeds...*All those single middle-aged white females?...*No unneutered males or... hounds...*Why hounds? Maybe because they bark too much... *Must make 2 ½ times the going rent...*If I made that much, we wouldn't need their stinking apartment...*show proof of income...*Most of my income is in tips...+ *$50 extra per each dog that is small & $30/ an application for each adult...*And with four kids, we're required to rent at least a four-bedroom. Or even a five-bedroom! I mean, wouldn't that just be a house? Or, what is it they call them—a condominium?...*No mixes of any aforementioned breeds!...*I have so many parking tickets now.

But, if we put the dogs on a diet, we might be able to pass them off as 30-lb'ers, even though they're wolf/malamute/shepherd/mastiff/pitbull mixes. No hound. But you can't prove that. Oh, I suppose they have those DNA tests now. For dogs. And humans too. I don't know my biological parents. If I did the test, what would they find? That I'm an Asiatic wolf/malamute/shepherd/mastiff/pitbull/beagle mix over 100 lbs? Then what would that make my children? They're barely heavier than a dog!

Couldn't they just overlook 10 lbs? I mean, we all do. Just this once?

Permafrost

7:25 AM

The front door swings open and shut. Three older ladies in polyester walk in and sit down in the Backroom on "The Mickey Hart." Which, you guessed it, is where Mickey sits, sometimes with his daughter. Tom Waits's son, the other barista, isn't working today. He once told me that when he and Mickey's daughter were at the private Waldorf school, he once accidentally got into Mickey's car. And now I don't remember, did she get into Tom's? That would be funny. Star kid swap.

In the almost-empty restaurant, the ladies decide to sit directly across from the winemaker and his lady friend with the beetle. I mean, I get clustering populations, keeping the open space open. But this is a restaurant, folks. There's nothing wild here except the salmon and even that is debatable.

I raise my pot at the winemaker with the question in my eyes. He waves me off. The hair of the old ladies reminds me of Frosty, a Keeshond, which is "a medium-sized dog with a plush, two-layer coat of silver and black fur with a ruff and a curled tail, originating in Holland," according to Wikipedia.

My face sags in the reflection of the computer screen. I wonder if it's the convexness of it that makes my face like that? Or, is the screen literally, in real time, making me sag? I wipe it down with some Windex. The glass crackles. In the

Backroom, the old ladies knit. They wind yarn, ignoring their menus. I sigh and look out at the mountains, the green peaks sandwiched in the fog. Its ridges are like bent spines cupped by the clouds, a swaybacked dipping. Large swaths of the mountain's foothills have been shaved like the legs of a large hairy lady denuded of her hairy trees, now sprouting stubble that will soon turn into grapes.

My children are wild turkeys, yo. They always know what to eat—the tenderest of shoots, the darkest of berries. The Roundup sprayers will come soon. The hillsides will be subdivided and developed. And then what will my children eat? They stuff weeds through the beaks of their lips. Purslane, sorrel, dandelion. Wild strawberries, their favorite.

"It's the braids," I hear one of the ladies saying.

"No, no. She definitely looks more Tibetan."

"You didn't think Nepal?"

"Prejudice is permafrost," David Mitchell wrote in a strange book I have yet to finish. Who has time for novels?

"I thought Native American."

"It's because of the braids."

People often say to me, *I like your braids*, and I'll say, *Thanks*. Because what else are you supposed to say to that? *I don't. They get into the syrup?* After work, I often discover that the tails of my braids are sticky. I will start to suck them clean but then stop myself because I have no idea if they've been dipped into the real maple syrup or the fake. Most likely, it's the fake, because the real we keep hidden. There's an up-charge of $1.50.

"But look at her cheek bones."

"I know, but the Native Americans have those too."

So, if 15% of $1.50 goes to me, and 2% of that I must give to the BOH, and another 2% to FOH, and the rest to the owners, how much does that leave me per a ramekin of real, depending if I rounded up or down? I always round up when I pay out. Some of my co-workers only round down.

"Did you know that our great great grandmother..."

The silica in the window's prehistoric glass migrates downwards at a glacial speed, distorting the mountains, my lovely ladies.

"What are you?" they both ask as I step to their table.

"I was adopted," I explain. "So, I guess, I don't exactly know, but..."

"Oh, really? From where?"

"Was it international?"

"If it was domestic..."

"That would explain the freckles."

"She could be mixed."

Perhaps this is when I should say, *I'm a homeless mother of four with descendants from Africa*. Because really, that's where we all came from, right—initially? Although, Korea is a pretty long walk from there, so, how did that happen? Land bridge?

"You know, Genie got a baby from China."

When conversations with the genetically-curious dip into the merits of 23andMe versus Roots For Real, or Yoo-gene versus Megene, I will excuse myself, which I am very good at. Because if there's one thing waitressing has taught me, it's how to end a conversation.

"Isn't Genie Jewish?"

"Yes. In fact, she is. Ashkenazi, I believe."

"Did you know, that Dad's Dad's brother's...."

If I floated on the sea for weeks on a raft made of discarded futon frames, or a sliding glass door so that I could see what swam beneath, or a mattress which I just saw on the side of the road, where might I end up—stranded on an island made of plastic bags?

"I'm sorry," I hear myself say. "We no longer carry soy milk."

The women look disappointed. Perhaps they haven't heard how soy inhibits estrogen production, or excels it. I can't remember which.

But if I floated on a raft for weeks, foraging in the seas, would I end up on some distant continent, like Africa or Asia? Or would I just end up right back here, and think I was in Africa or Asia, and call everyone Indians like Columbus? Although, Sundays are not good days for travel. I can never get them off.

"We have oat milk," I say. "It's the new best thing."

"I'll just take coffee," says a lady.

"Black," says the sister, staring, I believe, into my soul.

No-Milk

My husband, who I've often thought of putting on a corner with a sign, a hat, and a guitar just to see what would happen, identifies as an Atlantic islander, descending from many generations of musical mariners.

He tells me, "I can't busk."

I say, "Take a child."

He says, "I've tried before with a flute. Audience matters. No corners."

"How about the middle of the block?" He will play in a classroom, a concrete tunnel, a moldy gymnasium, an army barrack, for an ocean, a cliff, a cave, a seal—but no street corners? "Never mind. Forget it. I have a better idea. We'll sell milk substitutes. We'll call it *No-Milk: From the teats of gods who have eaten from superfoods across this globe and the next; from the mountains of the occupied Himalayas; from the uprooted acid rainforests of Brazil; from the seaweeds radioactively undulating above the bald head of Atlantis; from the dust of the soon-to-be colonized Martian soils...* Our slogan will be, 'No-milk! It's better than your momma's!'"

He doesn't laugh. He doesn't even crack a smile.

Outside In/Inside Out

7:40 AM

The second server hasn't arrived yet—The Young Handsome One (Ty Ho)—and I so need him to arrive.

I am standing by the swinging door with the coffee pot against my hip, which is a little sore from sleeping on the bolt in the back of the van that once affixed a row of bench seats but now only cradles my head. My braid is wound too tightly, pulling on my eyes, narrowing them. I have almond-shaped eyes, but I also have eyelids. Some Asians don't have eyelids—or, what's it called? Epicanthal folds?—and they'll surgically implant them.

There's nothing to be seen here, anyway. Particles of light flutter in the fog like bioluminescence in a cresting wave. A coffee cup tumbles down the center of the road. A middle-school-aged white kid with a piece of toast grasped in a paper towel crosses the street to catch a yellow bus captained by a driver who's never late.

From the outside looking in, the restaurant must seem like an inviting place, a heaven where coffee perpetually percolates and bacon always sizzles on a grill; a simple place where the employees greet you with a smile, and some of us remember your name.

The heat blasts loudly through the only vent in the restaurant, located directly over the server's under-lit, now overheated station. It makes no sense that Ty is late. He always complains in this high whiny voice, "I need money!" But he won't cover anyone's shifts. He never puts anything back in the mini-fridge and he's always in the bathroom. But he sure can carry a lot of plates. I mean, I love that man, but... As our old manager, who wrote poetry and dreamed of managing Starbucks, once said, hiring Ty felt a little like playing Russian Roulette. There are some people who just make you want to be reckless.

I shift the coffee pot to my other hip. The barista squirts steam from the espresso machine onto the floor. I squint at my order book to see what I've written, but there's nothing. Just some faint lines made by a dying pen.

"Ty better not have fucked up again," I say.

Outside, a Japanese American man sprays the ground in front of a newspaper stand with the beam of his flashlight, a Chihuahua snug beneath his arm.

I say out loud, "I have told Ty so many times, 'You're in your Saturn Returns. This is when your shit hits the fan. You got to man-up. Pull up the big boy panties.'" Is that a homophobic thing to say?

The barista rubs the nozzle of the steamer with his shop towel, up and down. A man crosses the street towards the hotel with a paper bag in his hand, stepping over some trash.

Ty thinks I'm mothering him. But I'm not. Against my black polyester skirt, I count on my fingers the number of years since I didn't have that first child as compared to his age and they're the same.

I place my face against the glass. "Come back. Please? Come Again?"

Lyme

7:41 AM

Listen, Shorty. Or, what do the cooks call you, "Chinita?" See all that pus? That's just the Lyme detoxing out through my skin. You know all that shit they say about how it has to stay in you for like five days, or that there has to be a bullseye? They don't know diddly. It can be transmitted just by pulling one of those fuckers out with your fingers. That's why I use tweezers. You should get some.

Here, I'll give you some teasel. It grows by the river where those mo fo's hang out—those little ticks. Japanese knotweed too. You know, hu zhang. I'll give them both to you. They're just at Jared's house.

Get some Tanqueray, some real cheap shit and make a tincture. I got red root too. You know, *ceanothus.* I used to keep it in a pot in the passenger seat. But I kind of need that seat now since I'm staying in my vehicle. I'm sure you understand. I'll give you all my plants. You got the bigger car.

It's just that last time I was at Jared's, he started tripping on me and shit, saying I just use him so I can park in his driveway, and why don't I ever sleep inside. I just sleep in my truck. But his house smells like shit, yo. It smells like a possum crawled under his couch and died. And then that motherfucker sat his unwashed 250-pound ass on it and squashed it. I'm serious. You know who I'm talking about.

He comes in and makes the whole restaurant smell like ass, orders all that orange juice. And then I got to open the take-out window and apologize to my customers for the cold *and* the stank!"

Sorry. It's just that with Lyme, I'm really sensitive to smells in the winter. Oh, and artemisia annua. You know, sweet annie? I got that plant too. It's just at Jared's house.

Floated

8:00 AM

It looks like rain. And how might that affect business? Might the second server, who is supposed to be here soon, enter saying, "But I need money," in a wheedling tone, face upturned in a prayer to the sky?

"Do you remember the flood?" Rosanna asks, while picking at a partially-eaten muffin on the counter of my station.

"Of course I remember the flood," I tell her. Unlike the fires, where evacuees must go out to eat—nowhere to cook—you can't leave home during a flood. So, on that rare occasion, we did close.

People often call us right before Easter, or Memorial Day, or the Fourth of July to see if we'll be open, and we're supposed to say, "We're open all year, except Christmas and Thanksgiving." Now we can add, "and, during floods."

Rosanna flips through her pictures and shows me a video on her phone, which she's not supposed to have out. In the video, her husband, who's currently being detained after he went to Mexico to sort out his papers, sits on the roof as the waters rise. He tosses down a can of beer to a neighbor, like he tosses burgers through our window when he's not being detained. A neighbor whom he had never talked to before sits in a canoe, hoping, I am sure, that he does not tip as he catches it. Because that would be some very gross water. She shows me another photo of the river creeping up her front lawn that she covers in our coffee grounds so the cats won't shit there, the cat shit now floating in septic waters.

"I was so scared," she says.

I nod sympathetically. She finds that photo of a photo of herself when she was nineteen, getting married to the man who used to cook here. She shows me a photo of her parents whom she will never see again because they're also in Mexico, and she can't go to Mexico unless she wants to never return. And then, what would her children, who are not quite citizens do? They'd have to raise each other!

"Do you remember when they stole our ATM?"

"I remember," I say, as I was the one who had to explain, repeatedly, to our panicking customers how we are a cash-only establishment without any available cash. And why we didn't have an ATM:

I said, "You see, there's this window next to the lockers by the bathrooms that doesn't lock. If you slipped in through there, all you'd have to do is unplug the cash machine, shove the flat part of a dolly beneath it like a spatula taking the burnt stuff off of a pan, then wheel it through the labyrinthian aisles of this restaurant. Our front door is just secured with a sliding latch lock or barrel bolt, like the kind you put on a chicken coop. You can almost unlock it with your big toe. Which they did. Pushing the door open with their foot, as they wheeled it out into the soggy morning, dragging the electric cord through the steel-hard rain.

"How do I know all this? Because we have it all on camera!

"So, if you need an ATM, the liquor store owned by the other Italian family down the street still has theirs, and it might even be working. Did you know that theirs was once stolen too? Someone backed a pickup through the glass door, tossed it onto the bed without even unplugging it, and just drove away with the cord flying behind it, the cash fluttering around like grass."

"How much did they get away with?" Rosanna asks.

"Eight grand."

"Oh," she says, as we stand there, shoulder to shoulder, gazing wistfully through the glass.

Death With *The Times*

8:05 AM

The swinging door swings open and then shut. I shiver. A black cape strides in, shrouding a man who looks like the Grim Reaper himself. He sits at my best table. Why do single dudes always have to take up whole 4-tops? He smacks his newspaper down hard. You can tell a lot about a person by where they sit.

But I am grateful. Because if Ty walks in right now, which he's supposed to do, Table 5 would still be mine. In fact, the whole right side of the restaurant is mine until C-girl comes and I lose tables 2, 6, 7, Back 2, and 3. Or is it Back 1 & 4? Then D-girl comes and I lose all Back tables. Then E-girl, and I lose some Out tables and more. So much loss.

"Hey. Good morning! Can I get you anything to drink?" I ask cheerily, as if this is the happiest place on earth, a real Shangri-La. He peers over some weight-loss ad with the before and after pictures. His cape hoods the top half of his face. "Are you cold? The heat should kick on any minute. We have specials today. There's fresh strawberries, blue..."

He silences me with a grunt, opening *The Times*, letting the front page brush the silverware bucket, a hot sauce, the salt, and some kind of flower in a small brown jar. His hood lifts, exposing a hooked nose, alluding to some eyes. And by the way he looks, I know exactly what he wants. I don't even need to ask if he takes cream. I lift the coffee pot off of my hip and pour, then set it down too hard on the table.

"My at-work baby," I say, shaking out my wrists. "I have my at-home babies. But this is my at-work baby. See?"

I pick it back up and cradle it. I smile. The heat kicks on. I look at his paper. *Mother and Children Drown In Vehicle During Flood.* For a split second, I imagine my children buckled into the back seats behind me, slowly drowning. *Ach.*

Perhaps the greatest gift we can give our children is to teach them how to die, to rehearse it, like a fire drill. So that if we were stuck in a car, per se, or a sand pit, or in an airplane about to go down, we could all hold hands and practice like we'd rehearsed, breathing, until we couldn't. Then, maybe we wouldn't all be so afraid.

"Do you have anywhere I can hang my cape?" the GR asks.

"Like a coat rack?"

"Yeah. Like a coat rack."

"Nope. Sorry."

He hangs his cape on the chair at Table 10 across from him, taking up two of my tables now, exposing the lettering on his black T-shirt, "How Will You Meet Your Maker?" I swear, this town is so weird. He sticks his leg out into the aisle. It's a fire hazard to block an aisle with a highchair. I don't know anything about a leg. If I hurt myself, my bosses won't give me workman's comp. I know because when I slipped on the no-slip mats connected by twist ties, in front of the dish bins, giving myself a whiplash concussion, I tried. They did pay for a few chiropractic adjustments, though.

Cook Time

8:17 AM

"What time is the second server supposed to come?" I ask the barista with Lyme.

"How am I supposed to know? I don't keep track of y'all's times."

The cook calls me over. "You haven't put in his food," he says, motioning towards my single dude now taking up two of my tables.

I roll my eyes. "He hasn't ordered."

Salvador pushes a two-egg platter at me through the window, sunny-side up. "It's always the same."

"What about my Back table's food?" I ask, suddenly realizing they're glaring at me without any food.

"What Back table?"

"The winemaker! I put it in like 15 minutes ago! Oh my God. I'm totally fucked."

"Him? No, you didn't."

"Yes, I did!"

"No, you didn't. I don't have Backroom orders."

"What are you talking about? The two eggs, toast dry. Can't you make it for me?! Please? Please? Like now? Real quick. I'll resend the ticket! I love you!"

"Yeah, yeah," he says, shaking his head.

And there's Ty clocking in.

"You're late. You didn't stock. We're out of Splenda. And we need more napkins."

"Good morning to you too, Beautiful," Ty says, smooching me through the air. "Food's up."

I grab the hot plate in the window with the red silicone square. I hook the coffee pot with my pinky, grab a water bottle, a glass, a pocket-full of butters, extra napkins, and a Ketchup, and walk my sunny eggs down the aisle just as "Love and Happiness" kicks in through the Bluetooth. My clog gets stuck in a gap between the no-slip mats. Although, I think they're actually called slip mats.

"Don't fall," Ty says, as I stumble, and a potato rolls to the floor.

Ty Stocks Napkins

8:18 AM

I love that girl but... Just because she's been here longer than me, she thinks she can act like my mother. "*Ty, go stock this. Ty, why are you wearing that? Ty, you didn't do your sidework.*" I'm so over this job. I'm gonna quit next month and just do the porn thing, and maybe date that rich fag in the city who said he'd pay my rent. Or move back in with my mom? Oh gawd, no. She doesn't love me.

They'll see. One day I'll be famous.

I hate going upstairs. It's so fucking spooky. All the cockroaches dematerializing back into the carpet. They do that when I sit on the stairs to count my money. That's why I don't sit there anymore like the other servers. Stupid bitches.

Those history nuts say this building used to be a hotel back when the train still ran and loggers banged whores for like $25. Porn stars make better money. Why do they always call us stars? We're not all stars. It's more like the Bates Motel here with moldy shower curtains half-hanging like a slipped-off bra. It's kind of weird how we have no idea what's behind the other doors, except room #6. Although the 6 is crooked, held above the door by only one screw. So, it could be a 9 or a 6. 6/9 or 9/6. The monitors are in there. See. There's the lights flickering beneath the door. But I'll be damned if I walk down that hall. I once saw a strange Asian-looking woman walk into 7. I never saw her again.

There's Room #4. Doesn't that symbolize death in, like, Chinese? Oh shoot. What did I just knock over? What did I need? Was it To-Gos or soup containers? Oh right, napkins! Was that really my sidework yesterday? Or is she just joshing me to get me to do her sidework? I'm so done with this shit. I swear, sometimes I just wanna kill my...

"The man is behind the machine."

What?! Whoa! Who said that?! "Identify yourself! I know judo!" Why are all the hairs on my neck standing on end? I just shaved. "Chaz? Is that you?" The new manager is such a dickhead. Now I have the soundtrack to *Psycho* in my head. "Chaz, come on. I'm just getting my To Go's for today. Legging-up on my sidework." Heh heh. Butthead. That'll rile him up. He knows I didn't do my shit last shift. He probably watches us on the cameras and jacks off. Why do people always bury the light switch behind the Barefoot Bubbly? Why do we even have stupid 187-ml individually-bottled Chardonnays? Don't they know how much plastic is in the ocean already? And come on now. Barefoot? In wine country?

"Chaz? Is that you? I hear you walking down the hall! Quit trying to scare me. Chaz? Chaz?!"

"...the...the machine."

Aghh! Oh my god. Oh my god. Fuck! Oh my god! What are those lights?! Am I dead? Jesus. Holy fuck. Did the paparazzi come? They blinded me!

"Chaz?! Chaz! Was that you? Please tell me that was you."

Shit. There's no one here. Why is my face wet? Oh no. Am I crying?

Alternatives

8:30 AM

"You forgot the Splenda, Ty."

"Fuck the Splenda. I'm not going back up there. It's fucking haunted."

"Whatever," I say, noticing that he's wiping his face with the sleeve of his hoodie, which he's not supposed to wear. Black T-shirts, sure. But no hoodies.

"We're gonna need Splenda. And you better have remembered the napkins."

Whenever people ask me for sugar substitutes, or ketchup, or extra hollandaise sauce, especially *our* hollandaise sauce, I am screaming in my head, "Don't do it!" Not to mention the sausage gravy—all a death wish.

Our friend just suicided. That's what they call it when you kill yourself now, *suicided,* so it doesn't sound like you've committed a crime, that you were free to choose death as your substitute, swinging from the rafters with your feet in the air. He was nineteen.

I make my rounds with the coffee pot. My children have known him for most of, or all of, or some of their lives. Or, how would you say that? Had known him? Knew him? But they know him still.

The dishwasher hands me more small plates. Last shift, D-girl said, "Mariano's sun is conjuncting my moon. That's why I love him so much." He smiles at me through his con-juncted moons, wide open and forgiving.

"My ex-wife thinks I look like death but I think I'm starting to feel a little perkier," my Table 5, The Reaper, says, taking his time with the paper. "Man, it sure does get hot in here."

When I top him off, he says, "Now you're my new best friend."

"Yeah, yeah. That's what they all say."

I pick up my tip from the Backroom and smile. The winemaker. Dependable—20%—like a fine wine.

"Don't worry about us. We're just ordering drinks," the frosted sisters say.

I open the old-fashioned oven, a classic white Wedge-wood where we keep the crayons, and pull out a coloring book. If my kids get dropped off early, I always hand them a whole coloring book and let them tear out the pictures of their choice. They'll study each page before meticulously detaching the one they want along its perforation. We have to pre-detach the pages for customers before it gets busy. It's hard to pick out just the right one a kid will want. Some even send theirs back, requesting Minnie versus Mickey, and then I'll look at the parents, panicked, because I usually don't have the time.

I glance over to see if the man with the cape is ready to pay. But he's gone! Where did my Grim Reaper go? Did he just vanish, leaving me to inherit his debt? Because that's what happens, you know. You put the orders in under your employee identification number and if the customers don't pay, you pay the bosses for it at the end of the day—out of your own tips! Why must they make us responsible for the transgressions of those who came before us?

Then I realize that the man with the cape has relocated to the Backroom. He sits beside a man in a suit who is talking too loudly to his compadres. The Suit looks like he's just been released from Bohemian Grove—a summer camp of sorts where princes and presidents commingle. But no princesses. No women allowed, unless they're serving. My young co-workers work there over the summers. They say no one's propositioned them yet. You get paid a good wage. But you can't have tattoos, dyed hair, or dreads. They never mentioned anything about four children, no home, or green-anarchist tendencies.

I once took my children to the harbor where one solitary sea lion barked and barked. My daughter asked, "Who is he talking to?" I said, "I think he just likes the sound of his own voice."

The Suit's voice echoes in the almost-empty room. *And then the phone in the hotel rang and I said, Sharon, Do you know what time it is?* Two women sit there listening to him, their expressions wall-like. *Not in Tel Aviv. In America!* The men laugh. The Suit shoots me a look. I go back to my coloring pages: Cinderella, Goofy, Pluto.

When we lived at the intentional community, my kids liked to watch the boy unscrew bottle caps with the tip of his bullwhip—his chest bared, a joint between his lips. Even my son, who could barely sit on his own, would raise himself up in his New Native sling as if he heard the call: *Hey,*

Bro. This is manhood, yo—mesmerized by the tip of the boy's whip flicking against the green glass, over and over, until the cap flew freed into the forest. There are beer caps scattered among the old pines that will never be removed.

… the place was infested with drug addicts and prostitutes…

The boy used to sit on his porch practicing knots. They'd watched him do that hangman's one before too, tying and untying the knot.

It was a fricking war zone. But a really great opportunity…

My husband said to him, "Hey, son, what you doing?"

The boy replied, "Oh, just practicing knots."

…so, I bought it…I'll probably build condos.

Our old ridge is still vacant of new settlers, yet occupied by ancient trees, and will probably remain so for a while. I mean, maybe we'll be allowed to move back after they sell it.

Or lofts!

Now I have a small stack of Disney characters to be colored. That should get us through the day. The Suit snaps his fingers at me from across the room.

"Hey! We want to order! I want a cappuccino."

When my children speak to me like that—declarative-ly—I ask them to restate in the interrogative. "Do you have a question?" I ask, but he doesn't understand.

I turn to the Reaper, formerly known as my Table 5 and ask, "Did you need anything else from me?"

He shoots me a look that could kill, reminding me exactly of my deceased great uncle who used to sit me on his lap and gouge the dirt out from under my fingernails with a tooth-pick. Sometimes, when I look at my son, I do wonder, how long does it take for the dead to return? Is it instantaneous?

"I need a double capp, no foam. And the lady wants..."

"I'll go get your server," I say, motioning towards Ty in the other room, our resident Greek god in black jeans, sucking on a pen.

The Suit blanches like he's seen a ghost. "Why can't you serve us?!"

He must be homophobic. I try to explain that this restaurant isn't one big free for all. We have sections. A-girl gets a slice. B gets a slice. C gets hers, although it's slightly smaller, so we rotate to make it semi-equal. Don't get me wrong, there's nothing socialist about this workplace, nothing democratic either.

I enunciate each syllable, to make it clear. "Be. Cause. You. Are not. In. My. Sect. Shun."

I rip out a few more coloring pages just to be safe. Families like to come on Sundays so we need a lot of pages. The suit scrapes his chair across the floor as he gets up, making me tear my page.

"God Dammit!" I yell.

He promptly sits back down. "Okay. Okay. But just tell him I want a double capp, no foam, and that the lady here wants the same. Low-fat."

I storm off with Pluto's ripped head flapping lifeless against my body, not mentioning that we don't carry low-fat. We only carry whole.

Entrepreneurial

At the intentional community where we all used to live, cottage-industries-on-the-land was a major preoccupation (now, for us, it's cottage-industries-from-the-van) because we, as a community, thought we needed money. When, really, what we needed was to just get along.

In the big barn, by the old mill site, where we used to hold our consensual meetings, we once communally suggested:

"Let's make ethanol from sawdust. Repurposed dumpstered bread for feed. Crocheted baby shoes, madrone stools, manzanita spoons, raw milk, knit hats, kimchi, dairy by-products, marijuana, hand-woven flax window screens, marijuana, honey, bamboo flutes, edibles!"

The boy, before he killed himself, made biochar.

"Let's grow hemp. No, lavender. Raise sheep! I like llamas. A doggie daycare! An egg farm. But the foxes? The coyotes won't let us go to bed. They peed on the mattresses. They were infested with bed bugs, anyway, Don't raise your hand. Snap your fingers. Don't clap. Hold them sideways, if you agree. No, not that direction. This direction. Not like that. Like this. What about a free store? Bunnies? Yes! They're self-producing."

Death on Aisle 9

Outside of the Community (If-You're-Wealthy) Market, the one that charges two-and-a-half times more than Whole Foods for celery, the children read library books on their stomachs in the grass, spread out as if this were their motherfucking living room. We go there because my husband likes to use their Wi-Fi and alcohol-free Sani wipes, even though their parking lot is always full. My children throw their sweaters onto the skinny limbs of new cherry trees in the market's edible garden. We are big fans of edible landscaping. All of their worldly possessions—glass beads, pine cones, carved sticks, yesterday's underwear—leak out of their backpacks that are set too close to the automatic doors.

People always tell me that my kids seem so comfortable wherever they are.

"Well, when you're homeless," I might say, "Or, home-free, as they're calling it now, all public space is your home, and time is your residence."

My youngest daughter lacks a filter. She likes to talk to strangers. She once asked a heavyset woman in the check-out line, "Why do you have so many chins?" She asked her doctor, "Why does your stomach look like it's pregnant?" When we were living at the Intentional-If-You're-Not-Wealthy Community, a potential investor in one of the community's latest cottage industries/business schemes visited us at our campsite where we used to live in canvas hunting tents (so, technically not "home-less", but not "homed" either, by some standards).

My youngest daughter was swinging, recklessly, on her rope swing. The investor was leaning against a tree where my pee rag hung. From too high up, she yelled at him, "My mother wipes her vagina with that!" and he recoiled his hand as if stung.

So, at the Community-If-You're-Wealthy Market, my daughter wanders over to this older couple and asks, "Why is your bag so big? It has so many zippers. Why?"

The woman looks down at her side-hanging bag, you know, like the bicycle messenger kind with the buckles, and says, patiently smiling, "This was my son's bag."

At first, the strangers are charmed. They're always charmed. My youngest daughter has this round sweet face and huge eyes with lashes that extend to her hairline like a grubby anime character (self-named, "Princess Dirty Face") with dreaded hair, barefoot, wearing mismatched leg warmers.

"Why did your son give you his bag?" my daughter asks.

"Well, our son passed away. So, I guess, now we have his bag."

"My friend just hung himself. How did yours pass?"

At first, I am alarmed. But they don't seem surprised. In fact, they seem encouraged and begin to tell her all about their son. How his name was Mikey. How he had a dog named Bodhi and had just gotten divorced from this really nice lady. Then, "One dark and stormy night," the lady says like this is fucking story hour, "Mikey was upset and took

Bodhi and drove away. They drove and drove right off a cliff and Mikey died."

Then my daughter asks, "Did the dog die?"

"No. The dog did not die. He's in our car right now. He just broke his leg. You want to meet him?"

At this point, I'm starting to have mixed feelings. Like, on the one hand: *Why are you telling my four-year old this?* And on the other hand, feeling like, *Yeah. Why not talk about death at the supermarket? Death at the deli? Suicide at the dentist's, murder at the laundromat, pandemics at the diner? And why not with a four-year old? Why not with my four-year old?*

I try to pull my daughter closer because maybe the woman is crazy, even though she is shopping at the Community-If-You're-Wealthy Market, that, thankfully, does take food stamps.

So then the woman says, "We're not sure if it was suicide."

My daughter gets this expression on her face like she's listening to Belinda Carlisle on the overhead speakers. The woman's husband mistakes her head tilt as confusion. But I know that look. It's not confusion. It's clarity.

He says, "I mean, we don't know if he meant to drive off the cliff to die," as if to explain, or soften, what suicide is. But there's no protecting these kids.

"If he meant to, he wouldn't have taken his dog," my daughter says and the mother breaks down and cries.

Ticket Dreams

8:44 AM

The motorcyclists have arrived! Or at least Travis has. The ex-roadracer/perpetually single and childless guy from one of the wealthiest counties in the nation sits at the counter. Regulars like that spot because they think they have better access to us as our station is right there, so that while they eat and we type orders, we're sort of staring at each other above the consul.

I take his order even though, technically, the counter is Ty's. In the old days, the counter was the free for all, the first-come-first-conquer-with-some-social-negotiations kind of zone. Free market capitalism at its best. But the new manager reassigned it.

"Can I tell you what I hate the most?" I say to Travis. His chap-clad legs dangle frog-like off the stool. I pull out a padded bar stool. It wobbles. I get off and stick a folded napkin under its foot and sit beside him.

"Can't you put my order in first?"

"What? You in a hurry or something?" I circumnavigate the counter and type in his order while he watches me through the screen's eerie glow. "Greek omelet, add jalapenos & extra onions, biscuit, no potatoes, sub spin." A car pulls into the lot and idles. Its lights shine through the window and into my eyes. Yet another design flaw of the location of our station.

"It used to be, Trav, that I hated being woken by my dogs chasing coyotes through the middle of the barking night. You know, when we lived in tents in the woods. Or the cold paws of a mouse running across my forehead while I slept. Or when a fox came right next to the canvas wall and screamed. That was crazy. Or really, the worst was waking up to someone peeing in the bed. Oh wait, here comes your food. That was superfast. But now, I kind of miss it. Except the peeing part. That still happens. In the van."

Most of the regulars know about our situation. They know that we're looking for a new place to live. Some know that we've been sleeping in our vehicle (the ex-motorcycle racer does). They all knew when the land where we once lived was sold, and to whom, and for how much ($3.5 million). Because it's a small town and everyone knows your biz.

Living in a wall tent is way nicer than living in a van, is another line I feed my regulars, *unless there's a wildfire*. Because that's what we did at the intentional community where we used to live. (Some of my regulars know that too.) If anyone accused us of living without running water, we could open the spigot on the steel tank attached to the wood stove and say, "See. It's running. And it's hot!" On rainy days, we'd cozy up in our 12 x 16, crafting. Then walk beneath a canopy of dripping leaves, down the hill to the community house at the old mill site where a then three-year-old of mine used to play in the wood chips, waiting for visitors—aspiring members, potential investors, WWOOF'ers, interns, researchers, trimmers, and couch surfers alike—welcoming them with the question, *Are you a magician, a musician, or a mathematician?* With her missing tooth smile and a *Be Cweative* button pinned to her tie-dyed dress, upside down, the dirt smudged across her weather-chapped pink marshmallow cheeks.

"You forgot my ketchup," the racer says, swiping one from another table.

"I don't understand people who put that stuff on their eggs. My dad does that. Have you ever read the ingredients? That shit'll kill you."

"I'm faster than Death."

A silver-haired lady limps out of the bathroom, trailing a long piece of toilet paper from the bottom of her shoe.

"Bye. Thank you! Have a nice day! But, can you, Trav, outrun a heart attack? Speaking of, where's all your biker friends?"

"They were going too slow. They should be here in about a half an hour."

"I better let the manager know," I say, not moving because the manager has not yet arrived.

"How's the house hunting?" he asks.

"Oh gawd. You know what I hate? I hate waking up with some rent-a-cop's flashlight in my eye, some uniformed sandman tapping on my glass. You know why? Because that's my glass. I own that window, outright. And then they have the nerve to give me a ticket? I should charge them for waking my kids—The Mother Ticket. More coffee? I mean, I bet it's a lot of work having a home too? All that maintenance."

He nods. "Yep. Try five."

"Oh wow. You have five houses?"

"Most of them are rentals. It sucks. I hate being a landlord."

A tiny tail of grilled onion hangs off his bottom lip. It wags back and forth as he speaks.

"I feel you. It must be hard. All that responsibility. Top off?"

"Sure."

"At least you got the motorcycles, though. Right, Trav?"

"The cops tried to pull me over again this morning. No cream."

"Oh yeah? What happened?"

"He made the mistake of putting his lights on."

"His lights? You mean his siren?"

"No, just the lights, just to let me know he was there."

"What do you mean? What did you do?"

"'What do you mean, what did I do?'" He mocks me the way my first-grade teacher used to.

"I mean, *what happened?*"

"I took off," he says, dragging the onion tail off his lip and folding it inside of a napkin.

"Oh right. Racer."

"Yep,"

"You dropped something," I say, pointing at the napkin on the floor.

Another regular sits at the counter beside him and I race back to the computer to type in his order. But the screen goes blank. "Boss man!" I call to the owner—the husband—who comes promptly, bending over with his headlamp on to fiddle among the cords.

"Mmm. Thanks for going down so fast," I say. He rises, red-faced, with the plug in hand.

"Hey," another regular says to grab my attention.

"'Hey' yourself. You want to know what I hate?" I ask.

"No," he says. "I don't. I just want coffee."

The Effects of Time and Water

8:47 AM

The door swings open and closed. No one comes in. Just the manager. He nods at his staff without making eye contact and sits down at my best table with his paper. He thinks he's early. He thinks he has time. But he's wrong. He's so late.

Outside, people scurry down the street with umbrellas tucked beneath their arms, fearing rain. But I checked the weather report this morning. The sun will be here soon. I scroll through my phone, which I'm not supposed to have. But, I'm behind the computer consul in the server's over-crowded, under-lit station, so he can't see me, right?—my face lit up by the glow of two screens.

Q: Do you know what's inside of me?
A: A whole ocean.
Q: What is an ocean?
A: It's the feeling I have for my kids.
Q: Who are your kids?
A: I don't know. But they're inside of me.

Love is a word like a pebble, like those small white stones people in the suburbs put down in their yards. It's only four letters. I have four kids, still living. That's why I say it's an ocean. No, it's bedrock. It's something I take drop by drop and dribble into their small bodies every moment, their momma-IV.

But you know what the sad thing is? They have no idea. They don't feel the sea rollicking inside them and know that is me, or the planet within that is them. I take that as my failure. Maybe I need to make my love bite-sized. Feed them in short sweet sips at regular intervals, pulverized and digestible. But I can't sugar coat anything. I put nothing on their spoons that's not on sale. For what are our children but traces of God, and what is God but in everything?

"Hey!" The manager yells across the room at me, which he can do because the owners haven't yet made their obligatory Sunday guest appearance. "Hey, you! A-girl! Where's Ty?!"

I slide my phone into the basket-for-phones under the counter, with the image of my children pressed onto my retinas like salt on a breeze.

"How am I supposed to know? I'm not his mother."

The door swings open and closed, open and closed. The customers have begun their steady march in, unstaunchable.

Smells Like Bacon

8:48 AM

I will forever remember that night at the Porn Awards. I looked so hot! I was lifting then and still on Atkins. I want to show you the pictures. Come on, look. Isn't that amazing? That tux was so wild. She really did a good job. And the pants! You can barely see the seams. Look at my hair. Do you like it? Do you think I should do it like that always?

So, I just want to thank you for voting Ty Ho, The Young Handsome One. I really appreciate it. Even though you will forever get gay porn ads popping up on your browser for all time. But I hope that when you do, you'll think of me. And if you didn't vote for me, 'Like' my page, hire me, call me back, respond to my text, tip me well, wait for me to open my gifts at Christmas, tell me you loved me, lift me out of the trash after you threw me in, call me when you were in town just to say hi…

"Ty! Are you in there? I know you're in there. Your table wants to put in a drink order and the manager's looking for you."

"Yeah, yeah. I'll be right out."

… one day you might regret it. I know I will.

Dress Code

8:49 and the third server is late. What's up with this Sunday? I claim her Table 2 with a water bottle and two glasses. Now it's mine. If C-girl does arrive, she'll have to wait thirty or forty minutes or, God forbid, longer, before I flip it and it becomes rightfully hers.

C-girl is the one who got me the job. We used to live at the intentional community together. One might describe her as "a big buxom blonde." She says she wants to write a book about those days. She'll call it, *My Polyamorous Life Among Members*. Or, *The Rise and Fall of a Western Intentional Community*. I said, "What about *Little Canvas Cabin on The Commune?* You could make a lot of money on that. You could write a screenplay."

"Good morning," I say to my Table 2, "The Winona Ryder," because Winona once shoplifted a salt shaker from it, although I think that might just be an urban myth.

A toddler wields a teaspoon in his right fat fist. The woman tries to grab it but he pulls his hand back, deftly scooping up a water glass with the other. He winds up for the toss, his pink cherubic face pushing out from his hood. The woman swipes at the glass. But she's too slow.

"Oh damn. I'm sorry," she says.

"It's okay. They don't break." I lean my face in front of the toddler's. "Go ahead, Sweetie. Throw it." And then, I get out of the way.

When my daughter was a toddler, she threw a fork at a ceramic bowl and it split cleanly in half, opening like a lotus. We called her Kung Fu Panda after that. Is that racist? My husband calls our kids rice crackers. That's got to be racist.

"Coffee?" I ask, pushing the whole pot towards her. It might help with her reflexes.

"Do you have anything herbal? Wow, I like your braids."

Beneath the computer consul, C-girl is bent over. Her butt bobs up and down as she shoves and shoves her bag into the packed shelf. Which we're not supposed to do because we might unplug the computer, according to our bosses. But that's not why all the screens go blank. They're just buggy.

"I'm sorry. There was nothing I could do," C-girl explains to the new manager as he stares at her cleavage. "I had to drop my kids off with my mom. She's two counties over. There was traffic."

She whispers at me, "Their dad's on parole."

"Oh, bummer," I say. We were all friends at the intentional community. Who knew he was so violent?

"You want me to take Table 2?" she asks.

"My Winona? I already brought them waters." So, technically, it's mine.

C-girl winks at me and sashays towards them with my pot.

"Yeah, yeah. Go ahead," I say. There are some people you consistently roll over for.

She pauses mid-aisle. "You know, when you're young, you have your whole life to figure out what to do with your crazy. But you don't know that then, do you?"

"Nope," I say, knowing that she's talking about the boy.

"What's that?" Ty asks, butting by.

"Nothing," we say, simultaneously.

"You can have my 15 too," he tells her. "They're fucking dick heads. The old fags are always so mean to me."

"Really? I love those guys," she says.

The owner walks in—the wife—and turns down the volume of the stereo, leaving the barista to croon solo at the top of his lungs while Bill Withers whispers about his lovely day.

The owner fluffs her hair obsessively. *Isn't C-girl supposed to be here at 8:00? That new manager keeps changing the times. E-girl better not be late today. Who's D? And, oh my God, Ty, No hoodies.* She fluffs while eating. *I feel like I've told you guys this so many times.* She fluffs while looking at her phone. *Don't you guys know by now, only denim skirts. And no leggings under your skirts, Girls! It's so sloppy!* She fluffs while seating. *Who's closing? I better not see any snacking on the floor!* She fluffs while chewing us out. *This is the last time...* Fluff. Fluff.

"There's nothing in our manual that says only denim skirts," I say because it's true.

"What do you mean? Are you talking about the manual I gave you like five years ago? Check the revised one, Honey."

"But I always wear black skirts. Celine never said anything about it."

"Celine? The old manager?! I fired her!"

Fluff, fluff. It's so useless to argue with an owner.

Waivers

The unborn are kind of like the breaks we never take. The baristas take breaks. The bussers break at the counter with their phones propped against the caddies. They laugh or snort or cuss as they shovel eggs into their mouths, swallowing without chewing. They take a bite of toast. Then, they sip their drinks. First one thing and then another. You can follow a life that never happened as it grows. Technically, if we work three hours, we're supposed to get a ten-minute break. After six, we're entitled by the state to a posture of repose and some sustenance, at a reduced rate—*there's no such thing as a free meal here*—to shovel into our open mouths. When they turn fourteen, they can apply for a worker's permit and become a dishwasher or a busser or a ticket-taker of some kind. At fifteen, they can apply for a driver's permit and drive themselves to school with you beside them gripping, by your head, the chewed-up plastic handle once gnawed on by a dog. If we don't break, our employer is supposed to reimburse us an extra hour's wage. That is, if we haven't signed the waivers, or fudged the break sheets. At eighteen, they will go away to, hopefully, the school of their top choice. If you've worked here for five years not breaking, you could be entitled to up to $8K of lost wages. *Goodbye*, we say, waving to them as they drive off in our old packed car. *Goodbye.* If you sign the waiver, or fudge the break sheets, just think about how much money you're waving away. At twenty-seven, they hit their Saturn Returns, which, D-girl says, is when, astrologically, your shit hits the fan. How much is a lost year worth? What about a lost life? If we're lucky, we get to use the bathroom, as the line for the only two toilets, grows longer and longer, extending into lunch, while the owners chirp like night hawks—*Sign the break sheet! Sign the break sheet! Make sure you don't forget!*—to further support the illusion that we have done something we have not.

Stop

The last time we saw the boy alive was during the fire. He was sitting in his car parked beneath the rainbow mini-umbrella strung up in the tree to protect the internet receiver, socked in by a smoky sky so fat you could slice it into strips. We were evacuating. We had woken to the sound of horns blaring, ridge to ridge, and the familiar smell of burning. We backed the car to the tipi flaps and opened the hatchback wide, sliding our most precious things into the maw of its cave: the dogs, the kids, a soccer ball or two. The children tried to put in their Razor scooters, but we put the kibosh on that. *Sorry. They're fire resistant.* We threw open the doors to the coop. *You're free! Go! Fly away!* The chickens hobbled out, tentatively, as their wings had just been clipped. We took the rutted dirt road down the mountain, very slowly. Because when you hurry, that's when accidents happen, my husband explained to the children. Every moment is a teaching moment when you homeschool.

The boy was reclined in the driver's seat of his Corolla, receiving internet. Maybe he was listening to *The Moth*, which he listened to often—that, and *Snap Judgment*. Maybe he was refreshing the Cal Fire page like the rest of this county and those neighboring it, so often that it no longer refreshed. I peeled down my window to say something through the crack, taking a drag of the air. But he didn't roll down his.

He only waved, turning towards me, briefly, looking grim.

But what I wanted to say was…

Get out of here! Leave!

Protect your young lungs and go somewhere healthier. Put out that joint.

Have you been sleeping? I don't think night shifts trimming at the grower's compound across the street is healthy for you. Or are you just taking care of the plants? Why not farm when the sun shines like the rest of us?

Have you called your mom?

Life is a gift no matter how it comes.

We love you.

You are loved.

Goodbye.

But my husband kept on driving and I did not insist that he stop.

What Are You Grateful For?

The owners think we're greedy, always trying to take advantage. *Of course, you want to go down to three, so you can take all her tables,* they'll say, when we ask to cut before lunch. *You guys act so entitled. You're so ungrateful. You think you can just eat on us?* they'll say, during those anxious eras between managers and before health inspections. *Throw away all mistakes. Don't give anything to the servers! Not even smoothies!* they'll yell at the baristas who then look at us, blankly.

But there was that time during the fire…Which fire was that? I'm not sure. I mix them up like summer vacations—Camp, Lightning, Paradise. The last time we saw the boy still living was in the middle of Paradise. Or was it Camp?

Anyway, some folks come to this restaurant just for the biscuits and gravy: Rosanna's biscuits split in half, laid open on a scorching plate, smothered in a reconstituted powder—a thick, creamy, gray gravy with chunks of the unknown and not-spoken-of mixed in. It's a huge platter, but we have half orders too.

When customers ask me if I like it, I'll say, "People love it."

"But do *you* like it?" They always want to know.

"Oh, hell no," I'll say, and they seem to appreciate that answer. But order it anyways, even if they say they're on a diet.

"I'm only trying to lose 10 lbs."

"Aren't we all?" I'll say and suggest the half order instead.

"Mas pequeña" indicating its size with my hands.

But there was a time during the fires when everyone felt gratitude toward the owners as they comped the meals of anyone who just lost their house. (Seemed like a bad trade-off to me then, but one I'd definitely make now.)

During some fire, a baby-faced guy walked in and sat at my small table. He said, "What rises from these ashes will be something none of us can afford." Or maybe it was the contractor who said that, the one who always gets the order of biscuits and gravy—full.

All that remain in these hills are cinder blocks strung across burnt lots like broken teeth. *For Sale* signs are more plentiful than mailboxes. Because even our wealthy can't afford to rebuild, selling off their empty lots. Working-class neighborhoods are being turned into condos, or lofts, their occupants evacuated elsewhere (gentrification being a different sort of disaster).

I see full-page colored ads on the back of *The Times*: A blond child on a purple Schwinn and shiny parents without helmets, wearing great white brightened smiles. *Welcome to your new home! A housing complex designed just for you! If you lived here, you'd be home by now.* I try to imagine this model family pedaling down the bike trail, cycling past rows of provisional housing constructed out of cardboard, nylon, polycarb, an enclosure made from stolen orange netting in which a dog stands beside an overturned tricycle and a partially-melted plastic plant.

It must have been during the last fire when the restaurant was filled with people who had just walked through ashes falling like snow. Everyone's hair contained the remnants of their neighbors' bodies or books or expired cleaning products. The baby-faced man sat with his head resting on his nest of arms crossed on my two-top. When I approached, he looked up, red-eyed and wrinkled, like the dead recently risen and hung-over.

"You look like you've been up all night," I said, giving him my concerned mother look, as if to say, You shouldn't be out partying during a wildfire.

"I have been up all night, and oh my god, I love you. You brought coffee. Yes! And you're right. I was up all night. On the roof of my parents' house with a hose. It was quite a party. My buddy and I. We were supposed to evacuate but instead we went roof to roof and sprayed everything down. The firemen saw us. They didn't say anything." He sipped his coffee like someone parched from without. "I actually think we saved half-a-block of retired folks' second homes."

I laughed and topped-off his mug.

"I was dreaming about this breakfast before I even came in."

"That's great, because today breakfast's on us!"

The old manager was comping the meals of every volunteer firefighter, or any kind of volunteer. The winemaker got his two-egg breakfast comped for housing evacuated equines on the undeveloped portion of the old Harris ranch. The Japanese American man with the chihuahua got free muffins because he offered to put thirty chickens in his previous large dog's large kennel after the woman in the barista's line beside him said she had cardboard boxes full of fowl in the backseat of her Oldsmobile. The ex-motorcycle racer and his Harley Davidson crew got free coffee just for racing around the roads and reporting incidents to the Cal Fire volunteers who slept in shifts on used mattresses in trailers on Mbob's leech field where we used to camp.

"But the damn neighbor won't shut off his radio."

"All the mattresses have bed bugs."

"I swear, they haven't aired them out since the last fire."

The baby-faced man said that an area the size of Rhode Island had burned. Or maybe he said that the number of people evacuated equaled the population of Rhode Island. I can't remember. I was never good with facts.

Condensation ran down the windows like tears as the owners rushed around with pinched smiles, their hearts bleeding because of the burning homes or their burning money that the old manager was incinerating with a finger-nail tap to the screen, comping meals. The barista with Lyme handed out leftover smoothies.

"He's adorable," he said of the baby-faced kid, dropping off a small glass of a leftover pink Shooting Star.

"So, what was it you were dreaming about?" I asked the baby-faced kid. "Come on. Anything you want. On us. Custom omelet, Crab Benedict. You name it."

And you know what he wanted?!—biscuits and gravy, half order, with an extra side of gravy.

The BOH was so busy. The cooks didn't even argue when I yelled for sides without typing them in first. In the FOH, everyone was talking to everyone. A dog lover heard how the Cal Fire volunteers taking up my whole section had saved an English Cocker Spaniel from a burning laundry room, and bought all their meals. The owners were so grateful for that one act of kindness by a regular that they mentioned it for many a fire to come, which became so frequent that they eventually stopped comping anything.

All That Is Hot Does Not Burn

Listen, Chinita. You know what else I got over at Jared's house? Well, I got a lot of things. But I think I have some of those black peppercorns. The Sichuan kind. Now that's the shit. That's what you need. You see, what happened was, in China, the river flooded every year, and every year when that happened, everyone always got sick. Too much damp. So they started eating these peppercorns and stopped getting sick. See, fire inside. No flood. Wa lah. Dries you right out. I'll get you some. Next time I go to Jared's house.

Background Checks Are for Chihuahuas

It's not like we haven't tried. We've looked at rentals. But to see a rental, we must park at least two blocks away. If we leave our wolf-dogs alone in the car, they howl and make the van dance when a lab waddles by with a jogger. We must first spot-wash the children in the public fountain. But my son won't go anywhere near water, not even coming out of a faucet.

"You know why?" I ask my husband.

"Why?"

"Land birth. He's the only one of our kids born in a bed, not a birth tub."

"Mmm," he grunts, familiar with my theories.

The first daughter shot out of me into the birth tub and floated across the tub, face down, arms spread, like a superhero soaring. At first, I thought she was a hemorrhoid or my spleen. But she flipped around and faced me, like in that cartoon, *Rocky and Bullwinkle*. You know how, in the beginning, Rocky, the blue squirrel, not the moose, streaks across the screen then twists to face his viewers. That's exactly what she did in the tub, and so I thought, "Oh. Flying squirrel!" eventually scooping her out of the water.

The second child's head came out slowly, hair undulating

kelp-like beneath the little waves. She slipped out behind me where my husband waited in his shorts. He caught her and passed her back through my legs in a reverse hike, like in football, and then I pulled her out. The third one sank to the bottom like a catfish, her cord slowly unspooling. I dipped my hands into the water, even swished them around, careful not to get my sleeves wet. But I couldn't find her! So my husband fished her out instead. The fourth one, well… Land birth—doesn't want anything to do with the water.

The first time we looked at an apartment, the agent had arrived before us with a smile that could be peeled off. I believed I'd waited on her before.

"Brand new," she said, gesturing at the carpets off-gassing into the 1200 square foot closed-windowed space. The youngest daughter smooshed her face into the wall-to-wall, huffing. The death of a brain cell is a thing to mourn.

"$1600 a month?" I asked.

"$1800," the agent corrected, tapping a painted nail against her chin.

"Brand new." My daughter pulled her face out of the carpet, giggling, cross-eyed, and crawled into the walk-in, declaring it her room.

"That's a closet, stupid," her sister said.

The agent smiled, or grimaced. I couldn't tell which.

"$1800 per month for a two-bedroom. You allow dogs too, yeah?" I asked.

"Yes. Small dogs. Your dogs are small, right?"

"Chiquitas," I said, pressing my thumb and forefinger

together in front of my one open eye.

On the highway outside the master bedroom, traffic backed up. Drivers peered into the apartment as they waited. My children waved. They slammed the doors—cabinet doors, bedroom doors, all of the closets. They found the hot water heater and screamed, "A monster!" then slammed that door too.

The door to a tent is almost silent, the swish of cloth like beating wings.

My husband stared at the fuse box. Someone downstairs was crying. I found a daughter clutching a door knob in one hand, the other hand braced against a recently smudged wall. She yanked and yanked, yelling, "I need to go outside!"

"Just push the lever, Hon," the agent said.

"Door knobs," I said to the agent. "I guess they haven't come across that kind yet."

My daughter shot outside like she once shot out of me, slamming the door into the wall. She lifted up her dress and pissed across the newly landscaped strip of yard, waggling her bared butt up and down.

My eldest commented in a valley-girl accent, "Oh *my* god. That's, like, what toilets are for."

"Have you had many other people look at the apartment?" I asked.

"Many," she said, definitely grimacing. "You'll need verifiable income," she said to my husband who wouldn't take his eyes off the fuse box.

"Most of my income is in tips," I said.

"That's not verifiable," she said.

"But I'm a waitress," I whined.

"I know."

As we buckled the little ones up in their seats, we felt hopeful.

"Well, that was a nice house," a kid said, and no one contradicted.

"Oh no! Shut the door!" I yelled. But it was too late. The dogs bolted out into the cemetery, racing across the green. They splattered urine across numbers on gravestones—a life reduced to an en-dash connecting DOB & DOD, etched in stone.

"That's one of the reasons I want to be cremated," my eldest daughter said. "One of many."

I had no idea she even thought about death. I yelled, "Om-a-ha! Trav-ell-er! Come! Come on. Come here!" No response. "Please?!"

The dogs got their zoomies on. They rolled across the Jews, the Catholics, the Protestants, the Greek Orthodox, leaping over their cool crosses. They returned, snarling, airborne, yanking on each other's ears, canines clashing. The biggest one, an almost 100-pounder to be honest, snagged the foreleg of his sister, and they both came down across the Chinese. Springing up from the graves, jaws snapping, they zig-zagged off among the dead, and I didn't call them back. I just watched them go.

Knock, Knock

It's 9:00 on the dot, and sure enough, there's D-girl clocking in right on time. I already put my waters on her table. So, her table's mine.

"Coffee?" I ask, as I pour, accidentally dripping on the customer's tattooed knuckles. "Wakes you up twice," I joke—the line that I feed them when I dribble.

But the big guy doesn't laugh. He doesn't even flinch. High pain threshold? An anteater tattooed on his neck sucks up little ants trying to crawl into his ear. Beneath the other ear, beside an earring that connects to his pierced cheek, a little monkey waits, plucking up the ants as they exit.

"Whoa. Is that a pygmy marmoset?" I ask.

"Yep. I even got a baboon. Guess where?"

"On your back?"

"No. I have a bonobo there. I'm a tattoo artist. Primates are my specialty."

He looks proud. In fact, his girlfriend looks proud too. She has freckles, almond eyes, long, wavy black hair, a wide face and high cheekbones—kind of like me. Her hand rests on his thigh.

"We want the double decker delight, with peanut butter on the side and extra whipped cream. Oh, and a bowl of oatmeal," the girlfriend says, ordering, I assume, for both of them.

"Do you want the real maple syrup or just the one that comes with it?"

The boyfriend says, "Nah, Man. Just give me that Aunt Jemimah shit. And I want a side of potatoes slathered in cheap oil."

"It's Log Cabin," I say. "And we use olive." (Cut with canola, or palm, of course.)

"Whatever," he says, scratching his monkey.

"Did you want to add any raisins and walnuts to the oatmeal? Or a side of fresh strawberries, blueberries, or raspberries?"

The girlfriend nods, wide-eyed and excited by my possibilities. "Are you Kazak?" she asks.

"Me?"

"You look Kazak."

She studies me, as if peering through the branches of my tree all the way down to my roots. I peer back. We look like we could be sisters.

She pulls out her phone and shows me a picture of a wind-chapped, dreaded-up four-year-old standing on a plain before snow-capped mountains, like an image straight out of a National Geographic. "My niece," she says.

I pull out my phone, which I'm not supposed to do, and show her a photo of my dreaded-up four-year-old in leg warmers standing before our canvas tent in Sonoma County.

"They look so similar, don't they?" I say.

"Like twins!"

The thing about not knowing anything about your birth family is that nothing that you have been told about yourself has to define you. Everything you think you know could be false, and the truth, which is unknown, is full of boundless possibilities. Everyone here could be my brother, my sister, all the boys my sons. My daughters—we are one. One family. One world. One love.

The manager bumps into me and hisses, "We're on a 45-minute wait, Sister. Stop talking and flip your fucking tables," and the idea of oneness flies out of both my ears without any monkeys to suck it up.

"I'd give you a tattoo. I work for waffles." The big guy grins, making all the tear drops beneath his eyes rise up.

"He's really good. You hardly feel a thing."

I imagine a map tattooed across my back so that I'd never get lost, never lose my home. But then, an awful thing happens. The map morphs into the color-coded seating chart of this restaurant. Each aisle becomes a channel, each table its own destination, each station—the barista's, the server's, the host's—a continent. The bathroom and the upstairs become planets. The ATMs are satellites and the perpetual line of people waiting for the bathroom—stardust. The kitchen, of course, is our sun.

"Chinita!" Salvador screams at me from a galaxy away.

"I have an orangutan. Guess where?" the tattooed guy asks.

"Aren't they endangered?" I ask. Because, just the other night, at the Community-If-You're-Wealthy-Market, on the television screen mounted above their kombucha bar, my children and I saw one orangutan momma holding her baby in a tree. We were standing in their edible garden on the other side of the large picture window, watching tractors buzz around like beetles, taking out the rainforest, raking the ground into striated lines to plant palm. I could hear the calm Englishman's voice narrating the event in my mind. But we were outside and couldn't hear anything.

"What are they doing?" my children asked, fluttering anxiously against the glass.

"They're getting ready to plant trees," I said.

"But there's already trees."

"What about the monkey? Where will she and her baby go?" a child asked, smooshing her face into the pane.

"Maybe they'll leave her a few trees. See. There's still a small patch," I tried.

"A few trees is not a forest."

"Maybe they'll rehome her," I tried again. Hope might be as hollow as fear. But what is the cost of no-hope? Suicide? Enlightenment?

"Come find me," the tattoo artist says, handing me his card.

He pulls out a napkin from our silverware bucket. A cockroach flips out of the bucket, skittering across the table. He rubs the napkin across his mustache while smashing the cockroach with his bare hand. "I do house visits," He says.

"What about van visits?"

"Chinita!" Salvador yells again.

I turn and give him the finger, the pointer one, that is.

"What's your name?" I ask, because there's no words on his card, only monkeys.

"Little Dot," he says, grinning wider than a planet.

Cold Waffles

9:10 AM

"Do you want my table 11?" D-girl asks, slathering her hands in Purell. "Those people had way too many children."

"You mean, 'have'?"

"No, 'had.'"

I look closer at Table 11: five little kids, and one woman. "All those children aren't hers."

"What?" D-girl pumps soap onto her hands, rubbing them vigorously for more than 20 seconds beneath the tepid water. Our bosses turn down the water heater so we don't use too much propane, unless we're expecting the health department. She dries her hands with many paper towels. "I figure, I never got to have the benefits of kids, so why should I have to deal with the drawbacks?" She glares at me through her glasses.

People often look at my husband and I as if we're lazy. (With four kids?) "Breeders," they might say, as if our loins alone have increased the heat of the earth and the rising rates of unemployment. But not food shortage. Because, really, there's no food shortage here.

"Maybe that one that just fell off the highchair is hers," I say, as another woman walks over, and then another. "Come on, there's only one or two per a lady!"

My husband, who is not adopted, started a band with his

parents. They call themselves, "The Conceivers."

"You take the moms and I'll take your other table, the one with the cute tattooed guy. It's in my section, anyway." She smiles, looking even more like a cat.

"But I already put in their order."

"Just transfer it to me." She scurries away.

"Good morning," I sing-song. The baby unsuctions itself from the breast and pops up, wide eyes boring into me. The mother, exposed, drips milk onto a fold of pale skin. She pulls down her shirt, seeming embarrassed or angry. Or sad.

"Look, Hon," I say, cupping my boobs. "This body has been pregnant and/or nursing for seventeen years straight."

All the moms turn and look. The babes too, even a few other tables. The mothers drop down on their knees. They wave their arms at me like I'm some kind of goddess. The toddlers too, the whole freaking restaurant, including the cooks. They throw garlands at my feet and tips into my cinched apron, applauding, *You're amazing!* What a *goddess! You deserve the best.* Or at least that's what I wish would happen.

The mothers, instead, look horrified. *They don't even milk cows that long,* C-girl once said. They scan my body, mentally assessing age, weight, height, wrinkles, white hairs etc. So, I segue into the specials.

"Today, we have a strawberry waffle, fresh raspberries on a waffle, and an egg and cheese waffle-sandwich with ham. That also comes with syrup. And a pesto-bacon Benedict. All our waffles come with powdered sugar and homemade whipped cream, which is really delicious. And, you can upgrade to real maple syrup, which I suggest. Does anyone want to start with a drink?"

I pray for sides of avocado per kid, espresso drinks with oat milk, Crab Benedicts. Up-sales on everything.

"Some lemon with my water, please?"

"Just hot water."

"I need ice. Please."

"Oatmeal?"

"Sure," I grimace. Trips made without any monetary reward. Possibly without any reward at all.

"Let me tell you a secret," I like to say to any table who will listen. "I never understood the purpose of enlightenment and those many-armed goddesses, you know, like the Hindus have, until I had four kids and became a waitress."

Usually, I am rewarded with laughter. Sometimes I just get blank stares. You have to know your audience. Context matters. But if they like me and they're laughing, well, that's a bonus. Something extra, as the Zen Buddhists say.

Behind the counter, in our station, D-girl is yelling at the cooks. "What am I supposed to do with cold waffles?! And this! This is not extra crisp!" She holds up a piece of bacon by its butt. It flops obscenely. "I have worked at so many restaurants! But this!" She slams the microwave door. "This…! Is unbelievable!" Her superwoman cat-eye glasses graze my cheek. We watch the numbers on the microwave ticking backwards.

"Where is E-girl?" I ask.

"You read my mind. You know why?" She makes bunny ears with her fingers and swishes them between our eyes.

"Because we both have Virgo rising." The microwave beeps. She grabs her weirdly-heated food and storms off to my tattooed table, leaving the microwave door hanging like an open secret.

"Chinita," Salvador pleads. "Please. Please. Run food."

I throw a random pecan into my mouth and chew. It's so stale. "Listen," I say to the busser standing beside me. Although, why is she standing? She should be clearing tables. "I never used a microwave before in my life. But, if there's one thing you're grateful for when you're homeless..." The busser bustles off. "...it's the microwave. Because sometimes, all my kids want from me is hot food." I find an egg crumb on the counter and pop it in my mouth. I'm so hungry.

"What is wrong with the cooks today?" Ty asks.

"If Whole Foods, I mean, Amazon, won't take food stamps for hot food, at least I can microwave it and call it dinner. I mean, if I can't serve my kids a hot meal, what kind of mother am I?"

"Amen," C-girl says, passing through.

On Table 11, the mothers are unpacking tins of pre-packed finger foods and laying them out on eco-friendly, non-slip rubber place mats like this is some kind of mother-fucking picnic.

"What?!" Salvador says. "You talking to yourself again? Run food."

"You're a good mom," Ty says, placing his head on my shoulder.

"Thanks, Babe. I love you," I say and mean it.

"God dammit! There's no Splenda!" he ejaculates, his

head snapping back, bent over searching through the sweeteners. His bulbous butt stares at us like a moon. I glance over at Salvador, and he pops his eyebrows up and down.

I grab my lemons, a glass of ice, a tea pot of scorching water with my pinky, the decaf snug against my side, and just in case, a straw, some crayons, a few coloring pages, and go see what I can do for the mothers. And then, I return and run food.

My Mother Says

"Food is for eating. Not playing with. Don't complain. It's too hot? Then hurry up before it gets cold. It's just warm? Great. Well, you're lucky it isn't cold. It is cold? You don't think it tastes right? Well, just be grateful that you have food and think about something else."

Like the day you were allowed to come into the restaurant before it closed, and only the cooks and the dishwasher were around, and they brought you a gluten free waffle—hot—and your mother gave you whipped cream as white and creamy as sunblock with real maple syrup—yum—and fresh strawberries sliced as thin as fingernails. All four of you each got a section, and it was enough.

"One waffle," your mother says, "is always enough."

When she sees you standing by the barista's counter, hoping for a treat, your mother says, "How'd you sneak in? Get out of here."

But you say, "No, Ma. You snuck in. I snuck out." Meaning, out of the van where your father waits.

A customer once saw your mother hugging you and yelled at her, "I saw you touching those children. You better go wash your hands." But you weren't dirty. You just came back from the fountain.

The cooks say things to you in Spanish that you don't understand, and things to your mother that she does. Then everyone laughs, and someone pats your sleepy head. You lick cream off your plate and your sleeves. The dishwasher, who has eight children, although most of them are in Mexico, says, "You're lucky your mother isn't stuck in Mexico, like Mariano's. He who won't be seeing her for a long, long time."

Your mother tells you that the dishwasher's mother keeps getting arrested trying to cross over because she wants, so badly, to be with her sons.

When you yawn, your mother says, "Go take a nap. You've had a long day." But how can one day be longer than another? Aren't they all the same number of hours?

She yawns back. "These days...They're just so damn long."

The cook asks if you play soccer, if you score goals. You say your sister plays soccer. She plays club, but she's on break now because her teammates play high school and she can't play high school because she's homeschooled. The cooks say you look just like your mother. They always say that. They never say bad things about her, which she tells you they so often do.

You ask, "How can you know, Ma, if you can't understand Spanish?"

"Isidro tells me. Isidro always translates."

But your mother once told you that the prep cook told her that Isidro doesn't even speak Spanish, that he speaks some unknown unspoken language from the mountains. You wonder about such a language that comes from mountains. You wonder about mountains that hide words, and what your mother does, exactly, when she disappears for hours, returning with stamped paper coffee cups of cold fries.

She touches the pink scarf at her throat and says, "La bufanda."

"What's that?" you ask.

"It means, 'scarf.' At least, that's what they taught me in high school."

You try to imagine your mother in high school—she's so old—while she tells the story of her day, how the cook said something to her in Spanish, and how when she asked Isidro to translate, he told her, "The cook says I should strangle you with your pink scarf."

As you fall asleep in your car seat, you try to figure out how Isidro knows what the cook says if he doesn't speak Spanish. How does he talk to your mother if he doesn't know English? How can your mother even understand? And just what language do they speak when they're together?

(this is not here)

this is silence, hon. this is white space. the sack I've sewn you, love. for the sound. for my old bones overseas. for what's not spoken, once named. my love is a tentacle, slicing through your egg, reaching through the whirlpool of your days, when I'm gone.

here. open it, Sweetie. don't cry. shake it. gently. listen for. here.

me. you.

to birth is to death drawn out. peeled down. walls. please is a prayer to a still smokey sky.

neck. broke. see, how the moon swings when the clouds pass?

where's mom?

at work. at the restaurant, pouring cider.

Too Late

10:05 AM

The man in the suit in the Backroom calls me over. Shouldn't Ty have kicked him out by now? He's been here for hours. And we're slammed!

"This one's empty," he says, shaking his salt at me.

"It's half full. Didn't you order the hash anyways? I'm just saying. It's super salty. Or at least I think it is. But I can't really take salt very well. Especially not just like, you know, Morton's. Oh, you got the biscuits and gravy? Even saltier."

I stick the saltshaker in my pocket, anyways, and walk-skip back towards my station as we are not allowed to run. *Jam on 10. Check on 5. Counter, coffee, salt,* I chant like a mantra as I pass other servers mumble-chanting the same. *Change on 9, Mimosa on 3, a side of Rye dry, counter.* I run-skip over two bussers, and a boss. Even a busser on an errand is chanting too. *Large OJ, side of ham, ramekin of jam, coffee.* We are planets orbiting soon to collide in a supernova of dishes.

"Hey, slow down," yells the new manager—so fresh like a baby.

"Excuse me, waitress. Do you guys serve hard-boiled eggs?"

"I ordered a cappuccino! With oat milk!"

"Sorry. The baristas are kinda backed up right now."

The barista with Lyme and the other barista, who is not Tom's son, sing along to the Beatles. They rock their shoulders back and forth, steaming milk as the line to their station snakes up the aisle through my station. I push through. The owner—the wife—yells at me to slow down. The cooks tell me to hurry up. The busser stands in my way. Everybody is cursing, bilingually.

"She'd be really good at roller derby," I hear the busser say of me.

Three of my orders are already in the window. I shove a more-than-half-full salt shaker into my apron, not noticing that most of its contents are grains of rice. I print a check and unroll it across one of the little metal plates on which we deliver them, deftly snapping a magnet onto it with one hand—print and repeat, print and repeat—stick a soy sauce bottle of cream, right-side up, and a stack of glasses in my pocket. It tugs my apron towards my knees. I tuck menus into my armpit and waste three unused napkins to hold my too-hot plates, making a busser follow me with a coffee pot.

"Thanks, Hon. You're a lifesaver."

"Food is getting cold!" the cook yells as his orders print endlessly, flapping past the kitchen window like dying birds.

"Apúrate!" I yell, but no one laughs. I step onto the floor, entering orbits of electrons warp-speeding towards death. I grab a stray potato and stuff it in my mouth.

"No chewing on the floor!" The manager screams from the Pleiades.

"But I'm dying."

For some reason, Ty is standing stock still, saying, "After

you kill yourself, there's this period of time when your brain is dead, but not your body. Or is it your body and not your brain? I can never remember."

I deliver waffles with extra syrup to the tattooed table for D-girl, pick up three dirty plates, drop some checks, make eye contact, resume speed, pause, take orders, flip another table, pocket my money, and go.

"Whoa. Slow down there, Speedy," the owner—the husband—says.

I fake smile as I check my dirty plates for unused butters before clattering them into the dish bin, turn quickly on my clogs with another scorching plate in hand, clomp away to set salt on the Backroom's table beside his over-salted food. He picks up the shaker and inspects it, shaking it gently. But I'm gone.

I'm in my flow now, frisbee-ing pancakes to the mommas and a few ramekins of extra whip too. I nod hello to an older couple, who I swear I know from somewhere, standing at the door with a side-hanging bag that pushes into a dog in a cast by their side.

"Enjoy the rest of your beautiful Sunday. No worries. Take your time," I say, when really I mean, *Hurry the fuck up so I can flip my tables.* A gangly teen pulls their leg out of the aisle as I hop over.

The owner always criticizes me for being too fast. He'll say, "All you care about is making money. You don't care about the customers." No comment.

"Hey. My toast?"

"I need jam!"

"I need more coffee."

"Do you have 2%?"

I run-skip back to the server's station to get everybody's preserves as we're not allowed to automatically put the thumbnail of strawberry onto their plates anymore in an attempt to make the $4 Costco jar last longer. But my coworkers do it anyway.

I drop cups with the mothers from another planet with their outside food.

"Sorry!" I say to the busser when I knock her over.

Ty is still talking. "After you've hung yourself, if you get resuscitated, you could come back brain-dead. Then someone will have to spoon-feed you and wipe your ass until you're old and incontinent. And you just die anyway!"

"Excuse me, miss? Do you have a moment?"

When the boy hung himself, no one cut him down until it was too late. Or maybe it was right on time, swinging lazy circles in the air.

"I always have a moment."

"Oh, shoot. I hate to ask, but don't you guys make your own ketchup here?"

"So why not just let people have the death that they want?!" Ty inquires.

Our alcoholic landmate who was nothing like a father, but the closest thing the boy had to a father, said, *It was a good thing no one found him until later.*

"Make ketchup in-house?" I say, incredulously, glaring at the crazy white dude like my ancestors might, because our catsup is nothing like the real thing. That is, the original

Chinese fermented sauce—so good for your health.

Excuse me. Sorry. Excuse me. I squeeze past chair-backs bearing platters above heads. "It's like working on an airplane"—another line that I feed them. Or, "I should've become a stewardess. Better benefits."

The young veteran of our most recent war tore off the back wall of the boy's house. Veterans always know what to do in emergencies. He gave him mouth to mouth until the ambulance came. It took them forty-five minutes. Can you believe that?

"Is this real maple syrup?"

"No. Did you want the real?" She never ordered it.

Who knows how long he was swinging from his rafter. Who knows how long his dog was howling in the car.

"I'll be right with you," I say to all my new tables, smiling with my eyes wide open so they don't get slanty, swiveling my head on my neck like an owl. If you squint, you get tipped less. If you're a woman—same deal. I'm sure there's a study about that somewhere. Although, I've seen it with my own two eyes.

I elbow past the owner to get to that inconvenient place where we hide the maple.

"I hope you're charging them for that," he yells.

"I need more butter. Sweet and Low?"

"Check, please."

"Coffee!"

"Do you sell this ketchup?"

"Where are my menus?"

"Someone told me it was homemade. I swear she did. She said you guys made your own."

I pause. "Really? I think I have an idea who that might be. But she hasn't arrived yet and probably won't be working here anymore."

Then I realize how I know the couple who is standing at the door—from the grocery store! I block my face with a menu as I pass by.

"I'm sorry. We're cash only. I'll be right back with your change."

"Why can't I have hard-boiled eggs?!"

"Excuse me? When you get a moment…" Says one of the mothers. "Can you refill my ice?"

I freeze like a loaded-down goddess bearing more than other people's plates and ask mindfully with intention, "Now, just *how* am I supposed to do that?" My moments are nearing extinction. But I have so much to do before they die.

She blushes. "Oh, yeah, right. Never mind."

I am weighted down now by so many water bottles, cups, large whole milks, a coffee pot, three hot platters, five checks, alternative sweeteners and too many menus tucked beneath my elbow, including a drink one, a dog one, but not a kid one. Sorry. We don't do kids' menus here.

Ty is still standing in the server's station. Doesn't he have tables? "If you came back with brain damage or something, you'd be so pissed. If you've decided to suicide and you've chosen how to do it and actually done it, you deserve to have the death that you want."

"Have you been to your outside tables yet?" the manager asks.

"I have outside tables?"

And just how do we want our deaths? Over easy, over medium, over hard, scrambled, poached? Poached soft or hard, maybe basted? Surprise me. What alternatives do you have? We have tofu, we have tempeh, which is like tofu but mixed with grain and fermented. Don't get it if you're not sure, unless you're feeling adventurous. But no. Sorry. We don't do hard boiled. Not anymore. You're too late.

The Damage Done by the Dog to the Cars

I always thought the boy would visit me post-death. In fact, I was a little offended that he didn't, until one night… but first of all, let me just say that it's only ever one of our dogs who does the damage to the cars. The other, the female, just likes small furry creatures—in her mouth. But the male, Traveller, has separation anxiety and he'll chew on things—like walls and furniture and cars—when he's left.

There was a seatbelt on the old Forester that we once owned before we blew the head gasket. And don't even get me started on the I-mark, our golden '82 Isuzu sedan with no available parts anywhere in this nation but still gets 40 to the gallon—"the poor man's Prius." If you try to turn on a blinker, the wipers come on. If you try to turn on the windshield wipers, well, just about everything will turn on, or off, depending.

There was that time beneath the king apple tree on a property with all these goats, where we were about to move. The children were picking apples as the goats came near, while the dogs quivered in the car like arrows. The windshield was cracked that day. The door never shut properly after. I had never superglued a goat's wound shut in a dim goat shed. But I guess that's what it was invented for—adhering skin.

We had just been invited by the owners to live there free of charge, indefinitely, and then promptly invited to leave, per gratis.

"You can stay if you drop your dogs off at the shelter," they suggested. But *Home is where the Honda is* (although, now we have a Ford van), and some of our family have fur. I mean, what would our two-year old think if she woke up one morning and two of her siblings had been disappeared? That she was living under a government-supported dictatorship?

The worst was the Subaru Outback. I had left the male parked at the bottom of our trail at the intentional community where we used to live. All of the windows were open. He was tied on a short leash to the back so that he wouldn't jump out of a window. It was winter. He wasn't going to overheat. But when we returned, he was sitting beside the boy in front of the boy's small house, stretched out like a sphynx. He opened one droopy dog-eye every time the boy hit the bottle with his bull whip, practicing.

"You should take a look at your car," the boy said, dropping his whip, which lay beside him like an obedient dog.

In the Outback, flayed strips of furry felt that once covered metal dangled from the ceiling. Plastic stuck out at weird angles like broken bones. The guts of the seats had exploded and bare wires bristled throughout the body so whenever we try to listen to the radio, one kid has to hold a wire to the metal to tune in, while another fiddles with the knob. And still, we only get Country or God.

It was the boy who always rescued a dog. When they escaped, he brought them back. When the female attacked the aggressive mini-dogs of one of our polyamorous land-lord's lovers, the boy grabbed the scruff of her neck and walked her home, leaving screeching dachshunds in their wake. When we went out of town, leaving a dog with him (the other dog was relocated elsewhere because they're easier to manage one-on-one), the boy even gave the dog a bath. The male is ferociously afraid of water.

And, like I said, I always thought the boy would visit me after death, and I was slightly offended that he didn't. Until one night, I had a dream, and in my dream, our dog, the male, is driving at breakneck speeds across a desert-scape, just like The Roadrunner in Looney Tunes. The children are curled, like spoons in a drawer in the car, back-to-back, still sleeping, while the dog races for the cliff. I scream and scream but no sound comes out. Then I hear a *snap* like a seatbelt connecting, and just like that, the boy is there in the passenger seat. He clips the leash onto the collar and says, "Alright now, everyone. Time to go home."

I say, "I should've known you'd come when I needed help with a dog," and hand him the wheel.

Cave Paintings Beam Light Into Dark

They say that you carry inside you the DNA of every child you've ever conceived, undigested. Whether that child was aborted, miscarried, or born and then died, parts of them remain. Small stones rattling in a shallow breath. Twisted ladders glowing golden, pressed into the ceiling of our cave.

We carry platters for our loves, the wound of our wombs held aloft.

Love isn't a color, Hon. But, sure. Go ahead. Draw it blue.

Somehow, somewhere, I still hold you. Somewhere, someone holds me. Bits of us (re)composting. Some things don't break down: microplastics floating on the sea, outside tables after weekend shifts.

You think I'm being too poetic, new-agey, pseudo-sciencey? Nah. This is Real. The neuropsychologists say so. The epigeneticists, the shamans too, and the poets (they were probably the first). A dowser divined it. The monks meditated on it, your midwife as well. They held your cords. The embalmers, philosophers, meteorologists, who knows? I feel it to be true. My womb is a cave, yo. Its carvings, glowing eyes in the deepest parts of the sea.

Undigested

10:55 AM

A blanket of fog cascades over the mountain and straight into our parking lot. The manager leans on the porch railing, calling out names into the mist.

Reginald, party of seven!
Billy, party of five!
Travis, party of fourteen!

I used to think that this fog would keep the crowds at bay. But, no. There they are, huddled in their North Face gear with their Contigos beneath the heat lamps, the week-end bicyclists in their flagrant spandex, listening for names unrolling like red carpets.

Sam, party of two!
Lesley, party of six!
Ansel, party of one!

How long will we keep the numbers of the dead in our phones?

I squeeze past idle customers bundled in their Arc'teryx with mini-dogs bundled in the same. One of them stops me with his torso and asks, "Can you get me a dog menu?"

"Your server will be right with you," I say, because I don't feel like fetching.

If I felt less barky, I might have remarked, "Isn't it funny that we have a dog menu and not a kids' menu?" The parents of fur babies would laugh. The fur babies of parents would laugh, thumping their tails against the porch. Do dog owners secretly wish their canines were babies? Do parents secretly wish their teenagers were dogs?

A single older gentleman waits for me on Out 6, sans dog.

"Good morning. Welcome. How are you today? Can I start you with anything to drink? Let me tell you our specials."

Some servers always greet their table by giving out their name, ie., *Hello, my name is ___, and I'm your server for the day.* But I don't. I prefer to keep that info to myself.

"Thanks. It's a great morning. It's my birthday."

"Well, happy birthday," I say, guessing he's around 87. "Would you like a birthday coffee? Or perhaps our special espresso of the day? We have a peppermint latte, an eggnog..."

He makes a face. "Well, actually, it's not my birthday. It's my daughter's."

"Oh great! Will she be joining us today? Shall I bring another menu? Can I get her started on something to drink?"

"No. Actually, I haven't seen her since she was nine." His shoulders droop. His mustache droops. His eyes droop, almost watering.

"I'm so sorry," I say, tearing up a bit myself. I put the coffee pot down, expecting some tragic story about the death of a nine-year-old. I have had nine-year-olds, will have nine-year-olds, still have a nine-year-old, at least, the last time I counted.

"Ever since her mother took her away. But I celebrate every year! She turns 44 today. I'm 69. That's a good age," he says, winking.

"You must miss her dearly. I'm sure she is thinking of you today, too. Even if you don't grow up with your birth parents, you still think of them often, especially on birthdays. You understand the sacrifice they made and how, really, sometimes walking away is the most selfless act a parent can make."

"What's your name, Sweetheart?"

My mouth opens, and my name rolls off my tongue, clattering onto the table like a coin.

"Okay, Sweetheart. Listen. Let me tell you a secret. You want to know what I really want?"

I pull out the chair and sit across from him. What does a father, who hasn't seen his daughter since she was nine, really want? How does he feel about his absence in her upbringing? Does he regret? Has it aged him? Does he long to reach out, conduct a people search? Does he feel that they are still somehow connected?

"Yes," I say. "Please. Do tell."

"What I really want... What my heart truly desires... Are you ready?"

I nod.

"Okay. So, listen closely, Sweetheart. I want the Eggs Benedict. But I don't want my yolks runny. I don't want them hard either."

The chair leg scrapes against the porch as I stand up. I re-balance myself on my clogs and scribble as I say aloud, "No. Runny. Yolks."

"Yeah, with crab. And I want my potatoes extra crisp."

"Extra. Crisp," I write, not mentioning that the cooks don't do crisp on Sundays, or that I too have a couple of children I never got to raise whom I carry around like an egg in my belly, undigested.

"Don't forget," he says. "No runny yolks. Over medium. Or over easy. Or whatever it is."

"You got it, Pops," I say and slip through the door, eager to tell my co-workers about the walrus-looking, fatherless daughter, and what he really wants. Because this is how we get through a shift—by sharing the crimes and regalos of the whole long day. But not the tips. We don't pool tips here.

Bite-Sized

"Good. He was probably an asshole of a father," Ty says about the Walrus-looking daughterless father. "What? It's true! My Dad was a prick, and I'll never talk to him again."

"Aye, Chinita, we don't do extra crisp," Jorge says, pushing a side of crispy potatoes towards me through the window. "Hide it," he whispers, and I do.

"You see this?" Ty says, moving his hands up and down his fit body, resting a palm on his ass. "This is all because the old man couldn't keep his dick in his pants."

"Shit, Ty. Just part of your 18 is up. You better run it. Do you want whip on your waffles?" I ask.

"Yeah, and the real."

"It doesn't say 'real' on your ticket." I grab a chunk of an overly-seasoned, too-hot crispy potato from under the counter and stuff it in my mouth, masticating with just my teeth.

"I know, I didn't charge them. When I think about what my dad did…"

"Are you gonna?" I ask, slightly drooling. "Damn that's hot. Because I don't want to get in trouble for giving you the real. Okay? Mmm. But so good. Are you sure you want the real?"

"… sometimes, it just makes me feel… you know…. Homicidal, or suicidal, or fucking… "

C-girl wanders over. "Check out my 14."

An old Chinese man stands in the aisle, bent over his table. An even older white lady hunches like a *Dark Crystal* character drooped over a two-top. Their foreheads connect above their plates. At first, I think they're praying—her, sitting; him, standing in the aisle.

"What's he doing?" Ty asks.

"He's cutting her waffle," C-girl says.

"What?!"

We watch, awed, as the old man slowly slices and dices while she waits more patiently than a loving sheepdog, staring at her food. From time to time, they both pause and look up to smile at each other, before resuming.

"Why is he doing that?" Ty asks.

"So she can chew it," C-girl says.

And then it dawns on me—it's true. Unconditional love is a waffle with homemade whipped cream and *real* pure B-grade maple syrup, made bite-sized.

I pour a ramekin of real and place it on his plate. "Here Ty," I say, "Take it. It's real."

This Ain't Fucking Goldilocks

11:30 AM

Time's flying, and I have no idea how much I've made. I mean, I have my goals. Don't we all? I track a couple roaming around the restaurant in their quest for the just-right table. They walk into the back, scan the small wood room with its big round tables occupied by people talking too loud. They turn around, walk towards the front, turn around and go into the Backroom again, circling like my dogs do before they lay down or poop. The manager follows them carrying menus.

Choose wisely, young Padawan. Because, depending on your choice, you could end up with the just-right table but not the just-right server for you today.

If they choose 2, for instance, they will get C-girl, who says that sometimes couples don't like her. She's too flirty. The women get offended. They don't know that it has nothing to do with their man.

"It's baked into me," she says. "I really should've been a sex therapist. I'd have made a killing."

If they choose 15, which they just might do, and they're homophobic, which they just might be, well, they're SOL. Because there's Ty following closely. They settle for 9, and if they don't mind a Korean, well, I could be the just-right server for them today.

"Welcome. How ya doing? Where you all coming from?" I ask.

"The city," the man says, without looking up from his paper.

"I like your braids," the woman says.

I put my hand to my hair. "I like yours too," I say.

Her hair is like sparse platinum feathers. The man lifts up his Porsche insignia-ed hat to reveal absolutely no hair whatsoever—immaculately bald. I laugh too loudly. Tears spring to my eyes. I can't stop. He looks offended. I'm not laughing at him because of his lack of hair. I'm laughing because I'm imagining him with hair.

"It's not that... It's just, you know... One day you will have hair again. We always get a second chance at hair?" He looks thoroughly offended now. How to explain that I wasn't talking about hair plugs. "I meant, in your next life. Or even after death, you know. It just keeps growing. Like in the grave?" Ty turns from the next aisle over and winks at me. He has a nose for whenever I'm sticking my foot in my mouth, struck down by the absurdity of life, or low blood sugar. So, I segue into the specials.

"Today we have eggnog lattes, peppermint lattes but not pumpkin. That's only near Thanksgiving. We also have mocha biancas as well as regular mochas." He scowls and returns to his real estate ads. "Or just coffee?"

"Now you're talking," he says, raising his mug.

I pour carefully, trying very hard not to spill.

"Now you're my new best friend."

"Yeah, that's what they all say just because I have the

coffee. You know, I always wondered, if I walked out of this restaurant right now, would people flock to me, yelling, 'I love you! I worship the ground on which you walk!' Or would they think I was crazy, chasing them down with my pot, pleading, 'Don't you love me? Aren't we friends? Aren't you so happy that I came?'"

But he doesn't even look up. He just keeps scouring his ads.

Context Matters

We used to have this one cook. Armando, was his name. He always opened because he had to leave early to go to his other job at Hooters. All of the BOH had at least one other job, usually three. He liked to take selfies, naked from the top of his pelvis up. He was incredibly ripped. He had the whitest teeth. He'd show us his photos when it was so slow, we'd look at anything. Even the cooks looked. No one cared. No one looked away when he'd start doing some outrageous dance moves by the broiler.

"It's like having a Chippendale dancer in your kitchen," C-girl said, peering through the window where the food came out.

"I bet that's somebody's fantasy," I said.

He wasn't a bad cook. He could translate the shorthand of each server's modifications. Cream OS, or Sour On S, or SOS, or SP, or 1 plate, or plate no! Each girl had their own acronyms. I don't remember if he was slow or not. Slowness is not something I remember about him. He was usually pretty even-keeled. He had one daughter, a steady partner, an old car. But then he tried to strangle the other cook, whom we all have dreamt of strangling. And, well, that was the end of his job.

At the End of His Knife

11:45 AM

The owner walks over—the husband. "What are you guys talking about over here? It better be about work. Hey, I hope you charged for that maple syrup."

"Who, me?" I say.

"Yeah, you. I saw you. Have you gone to your outside table?"

"Have you gotten us adult diapers?" It's an old request.

He rolls his eyes.

"Workers rights, Man. I'm just saying."

He noses around, investigating for mistakes left in our station to chew us out about or chew on: undeliverably cold waffles, charred burgers, burrito bowls smothered in salsa for a customer with a tomato allergy that we'll shovel into our mouths before hitting the floor.

"Aren't you the little Speedy Gonzales making all the mistakes? You better not be giving my customers bad service just because you wanna make more money."

"The only mistakes I've made are with their father," I say. Ty guffaws, which just eggs me on. "I know at least three of yours." We all look over at his daughter clomping across the hardwoods like a horse in heels.

"Shush," C-girl says loudly.

The owner laugh-snorts and goes to bug the baristas for

an ice cream cone.

"You gotta love that man," C-girl says.

"Yeah. Like a venereal disease," says Ty.

The barista with Lyme is bent over the fruit drawer.

"I need some ice cream," the owner says.

"God dammit," the barista grumbles about the too-hard fruit or the owner, wielding a frozen banana at the end of his knife. He's been cursing a lot lately. "Wintertime," he says. "My Lyme flares up. Lowers my tolerance for bullshit."

The printer spills drink orders out to the floor. The barista says he has PTSD just from the sound of a printer. I bet the cooks have that too.

The barista beside him with anger issues, or something, yells, "Fucking decaf drinkers. Stick a finger in my bung hole!" Another hired mistake. But what can you do when the employees keep dropping like flies? The owner squeezes by him, reaching for a sugar cone, bumping him. "Bung-lickers!"

This is why we turn the music up, not down, I try to tell the owners. This is why you need to put Tom's son on weekends.

"Mistake," I say to C-girl, covering my mouth as I chew, pointing at a small plate of cold scrambled eggs.

"Oh, hell yeah," she says, digging in.

I cram rubbery egg crumbles into my mouth, willing them to fill up the cavern of my stomach. I grab a fistful before heading out to my new tables.

The new manager stops me. "No chewing on the floor!"

I stuff the remaining bits from my fist into my mouth.

The owner saunters over. "Where'd you get those eggs?"

"What eggs?" I say, my mouth still full.

The owner picks a yellow clump off my shirt with the hand that's not holding an ice cream cone.

"Hey!" I spew. "Don't touch me there."

"Where'd you get those eggs? Were they one of your mistakes?"

He looks towards Salvador through the window. Salvador says, "I didn't give them to her."

"I took it off of someone's plate," I lie, pointing at the dish bins filled with half-eaten breakfast burritos and more sliced sausages rolling around than I'd like to think about.

"You ate it off a customer's plate?! That's how you get the bird flu. Or the bat flu. Or whatever flew over from your country."

"Racism!" I yell, ejecting the last bits of egg onto his shoe.

"Oh, come on now. Swallow!"

"Sexual harassment! Lawsuit! Discrimination!" I scream, as I scuttle over to the rest of my tables.

Patchy Skies Worn Over

11:56 AM

"Dude. I seriously have to pee."

"Me too."

"Go outside behind the kitchen. I'll run your food if it comes up."

"Thanks."

I push past the eternal line of customers waiting impatiently for the one bathroom, the other now clogged, dropping checks as I go. I slip through the narrow kitchen, behind the back of the house, past the freezers, the heating/cooling unit whirring, and the ice maker. I tip-toe across a slick cigarette butt-littered strip of packed dirt and settle into a tiny space between the building and the fence. It's a well-worn path.

I pull up my skirt, carefully, cradling in my palm my order book still in my apron, crammed with cash. The clouds move purposefully across the sky. I wonder what my children are doing now. I pull up my panties, now damp, and ask out loud, "Is this really the best use of my time? Please, God, let it be."

Then, I retrace my steps to my station.

Friedman's, Some Nights

She sits on the porch swing in the garden section of some hardware store, the scuffed tip of her shoe touching linoleum. She pushes herself as she reads. My second daughter, the avid reader.

"Time to go," I say to the reader. "Let's go. We need to find a place to park for the night."

By 5 o'clock, all the spaces in front of the skate park, where the decent bathrooms are, will be occupied by painted-over school buses, as it's illegal to drive them still yellow. But whenever we park there, the children want to go out for breakfast at the overpriced omelet place in the morning.

"I wish there was time to read outside of time," my daughter says. She swings towards me. Her finger holds her place in her book. She swings away and opens the book back up.

"Come on. Let's go. We have to get the rest of them." The baby sighs pleasantly in his sleep, strapped to my body. His weight pulls on my shoulders, reminding me that he's there.

The fifth-wheels and new RVs will have already set up shop on the well-swept lots of the mini mall hosting a 24-Hour Fitness and Whole Foods, which has celery for $2.49 a bunch. There's a Honey Bucket there in their parking lot. But my children prefer the bushes. "But if you have to poop," I tell them.

"Huh?" the reader says, still reading.

The Grocery Outlet by the bike path sells celery for $.99 a pound. But if we park there, we're surrounded by dented vans donning old sheets over their windows, squawking like nighthawks through my sleepless night. Squeaky doors that open and shut, open and shut, as folks go out to pee and receive/pass along legal/illegal drugs. Drunks, unhinged, sing like nightingales. Old condoms and needles hide in the rosemary.

"Where's your father? How come whenever we go to these stores, I lose him? We don't even have a home to improve. Go tell your father that. And, 'It's time to go!' Oh my god. Now they're playing Tom Petty? For crying out loud."

I want to have a night where I put my head down and never pick it up, until the light is fine lichen and the birds are silent, done singing. I want a night where the only thing that is memorable are my dreams. But lately, that's not how these things go. It's car stereos, marijuana smoke, and cursing—like a fucking state park campground. When I take my son out to pee, we look at the moon.

"Oh, *Little Women*. I remember reading that."

"Just swing and read, swing and read," she sing-songs, still reading.

Bullet Time

12:01 PM

The Suit in the backroom yells into the main dining hall, "Hey, faggot!"

I believe Ty finally told him to leave. The Suit repeats himself and the din of the restaurant turns *en diminuendo*. It's a *Matrix* moment. You know, that movie with Keanu Reeves? It's too bad what happened to his family. Utensils clatter against plates. Servers move in slow-mo in the background. The Suit opens and closes his mouth, saying more inappropriate things, spitting out vile language that I will not type onto the page. That I will not put into being. However, there it is, coming out of the big man's mouth.

Cut to Ty looking pretty hot. His jawline flexes as he chews on the end of his pen, laughing with some older women ordering. He runs his fingers through his finely gelled hair, ignoring the language flying at him from the bright red square of the man's mouth.

Now everything moves in slow-mo. Ty raises his head, vertebra by vertebra, turning slightly towards his assailant. He swings it back towards me watching him from across aisles. We lock gazes. I wink. Time resumes and the din of the restaurant turns *il forte*.

"I will be right with you," Ty calls over to The Suit in a calm and orderly manner.

The Suit, who I believe had too many bloody beers (that's beer with Bloody Mary mix and a sad piece of celery), or mimosas (with Barefoot Bubbly and fresh squeezed OJ), clenches his fists. Turning maroon, he stomps over like an irate child about to sock Ty a good one.

I wiggle my nose like Samantha in *I Dream of Jeannie*—except I have black braided dreads—feeezing the homophobe in his frame. Cut to the busser doing his Gumby-walk down the warped wood floor, carrying a dish bin, which he's not supposed to do. You can't have dish bins on The Floor. It's a health code thing. He's supposed to clear the tables plate by plate, taking them by the armload to the bins behind the server's station near the no-slip mats.

Rosanna clanks cups into his bin, being helpful. The Gumby-bouncing busser balances on the balls of his feet. He turns sideways with his bin to squeeze past Ty, who somehow always takes up too much space. It's his ass. He has a really big ass. As the busser brings the bin around, he lands funny on his toes, placing them too hard in the aisle. He trips, ejecting chewed-on omelets, melted smoothie, eggnog lattes, all over the man in the suit.

I waggle my nose, and time resumes. Glasses clatter to the floor. The Suit curses, smattered and splattered in red, white, and pink. Ty finishes taking his order and we all return to our stations as the new manager jogs over.

A Conversation I Wish We Had

Me: I'm so sorry, Ty. I didn't know it was like that. Why didn't you say anything? You should've told me. Why didn't you just come over? I should've called you. You should've come over. I should've called you. You can always call me, you know.

Ty: I did. You didn't answer.

Me: Oh, right. I forgot. They turned off my phone.

Coconut Matcha Latte

12:02 PM

We're officially on lunch, and the Matcha Latte Woman has arrived! I head over there with a bottle of water, one cup, and no coffee pot, so I have nothing to cradle except the glass bottle. Her long red hair lays in squiggles down the back of her seat.

I vaguely know the Matcha Latte Woman from outside of work. She went to high school with my husband, who said that her ex was an abusive man. I set down her cup.

"What was that all about?" she asks.

"Oh, just other people's issues."

The Matcha Latte Lady told me that the night before the fires, before their house burnt down, her daughter woke up from a nightmare, screaming, "It's burning! It's burning!" little whips of hair sticking to her sweaty face as she sobbed. "And they set the fires on purpose!" Everybody has their theories.

"How's it going? You guys find a place yet?"

She shakes her head, "No. You?"

I shake mine too. "How's your daughter?"

"Okay," she answers, but it sounds more like a question. "How's the homeschooling going?"

I lean against her empty chair. "Oh, I don't know. They're always learning, you know. Yesterday my nine-year-old asked me, 'Why do they say, *it's* raining? What is *it* anyways?' She can't read yet. But she's very observant."

"I couldn't do it."

"What? Homeschool? My husband does most of it. I'm usually here or at the chiropractors or acupuncturist trying to recover from this job. Haha. My husband doesn't work. I mean, unless you count homeschooling, coaching soccer, trying to make it as a musician, doing all the paperwork for a family of six so we can keep getting benefits even without an address. Not to mention the doctor's appointments. And the dentist's. My god. That's the main reason I stopped having more kids. I just felt like I could not brush another set of teeth."

"I feel you on that one. Even one is enough."

"Well, not to mention our own. I mean, I don't see how people can work full-time and be anything other than employees. Like, how do two working parents ever get to be parents?"

"Did you hear what happened to that woman from the Buddhist temple and her two kids during that last heavy rain?" she asks.

"How they drowned?"

"Yeah. I keep a small hatchet in my car now, just in case."

I think of the headlines on *The Times* in the Grim Reaper's paper. "Don't you think we should teach our children how to die beforehand? I mean, think of all the things we prepare them for that might not ever happen, like college." I try out my fire drill theory on her, but she just stares at me blankly, blinking hard a couple of times.

"Matcha Latte. With coconut milk, right?"

She nods.

I release her water bottle to the table. On second thought, I pick the bottle back up and tilt, pouring water into her glass, something I never ever do for a customer.

A Conversation While Driving With a Teen

"Marti returned to practice yesterday."

"Oh good, I was wondering what happened to them."

* * *

"They got arrested two days after Christmas, trying to jump off the Golden Gate Bridge."

"What?!"

* * *

"Yeah, they had to take them off in handcuffs."

"Holy… Oh, I'm so sorry to hear that."

* * *

"I had just texted them Christmas Eve, and said, 'I could see you jumping off a bridge. In fact, I could see you jumping off the Golden Gate Bridge.' I mean, I didn't think they would actually do it."

"It's not your fault, Sweetie. Marti obviously has a screw loose."

131

* * *

"Yeah, after seven days of not sleeping!"
"That'll loosen 'em."

* * *

"You should invite them to hang out sometime... I don't see what you got against the pool showers. At least you'd be clean."

* * *

"It's not my responsibility to keep my friends from dying, you know."

* * *

"Of course not, Honey. That's not what I'm saying. I'm just saying, you should invite them over. Sometimes it helps to hang out with someone else's family. A different context, you know. Gives some perspective. They could come meet us at the playground by the bike trail? We could BBQ? They could push the baby on the swing?"

* * *

"It's just hard for a mother. You want to open your arms to every suffering child."

***

"Yeah. Well. Whatever."

What I Should've Said Is

"You're Beautiful," or, "I understand," or, "I love you."

Or, "You can say 'no.'"

Or, "If it's not a 'yes,' then that's a 'no.'"

"You are not a bad person."

"There is a piece of God, or source, or Universe, or whatever you want to call it, in all of us. In that way and in many ways, we are all very much the same."

"Self-love and compassion, that's all I want you to take from this."

"You can call me whenever you need, even collect."

"Always scan a room before you leave it, to make sure you don't forget anything."

"When you're dying, focus on your breath. It will help with the transition."

"Whatever you do, don't let fear be your driver."

Instead, what I say, as I hand them their bowls, is, "You get what you get and you don't get upset." But they know that one already.

Pasteurized

12:15 PM

A couple sits peacefully in the corner. I can always tell when a woman is newly pregnant. Not by how she looks, but by how she orders.

"I'll have an American burger please."

"Do you want that with French fries, potato salad, or coleslaw?"

"Is the potato salad cooked?"

"Some of it."

"And the coleslaw?"

"I think coleslaw is always raw."

"So it's not pasteurized?"

"Raw, I believe, is the opposite of pasteurized."

"Okay, I'll have the French fries. And some juice. Is your Goodness Greens pasteurized?"

"All of the juices from the juice bar are fresh-squeezed."

"Okay, then not pasteurized."

"That's right. Raw."

"How about the fresh-squeezed orange juice?"

"Also raw."

"I'll have a glass of milk then."

"That's pasteurized. Do you want a large or a small?"

"Small, please."

"And, how do you like your burger? Oh, wait. Don't tell

me. Well done."

That is usually the way the conversation goes, with the newly impregnated looking to her partner after each question that I ask. I mean, I understand. I've been pregnant many times. Some live births, some still, some not even births at all. But when I was pregnant with my oldest, I remember being in a very hot bath thinking, Am I going to make my child retar... I mean, mentally divergent or alternatively-abled, or, learning different. Or, really, Am I going to fuck up my child? I mean, that's always the question, **Am I going to fuck up my child?** Reminding myself that being differently-abled or challenged mentally is not reflective of a state of fuckedup-ness. That's just culture speaking. But, really, that's beside the point. Because with every decision I make, I still ask, **Am I going to fuck up my child?** For instance, do I give them the gluten free waffle or the wheat one? Which will fuck them up more? Do I let them get away with not writing thank you notes? Or do I force them? Which will fuck them up more?

A customer once said to me, "But that's our job."

However, in other cultures, take Japan for instance, pregnant women, I believe, still eat their sushi raw and take their baths hot. I mean, I know I did.

I Am the Egg Woman,

choo, choo, cha, choo.

12:19 PM

A woman walks into the restaurant with a small dog draped over her shoulder. She surveys the counter as if she's looking for someone and spies the motorcycle racer sipping his 16th or so cup of coffee. A potential renter? The crowd parts for her and her dog. *Now that's the kind of pet I need.*

I make a fast lap around the restaurant, grabbing all of my checks. My time is running out. I can feel it. Suddenly, I'm seized with a chest-collapsing panic. Oh no! I forgot about my Out 6! The old walrus-looking, daughter-less father, extra crisp! I go outside onto the front porch. The air feels heavy with rain. His plate is still there: crab Benedict, mostly-eaten, potatoes drowning in egg yolk. His coffee cup is upside down. But I don't see his bald head, his long face, those eyes! Or, wait. Is that him running across the street? No, it's that weird guy in the long cape. Why is he still here? And I think, "Oh shit. Did my Out 6 just dine and ditch? Is that what he did to his daughter?" I pick up his plate and underneath there is a bill—a Franklin! Wow.

I try to imagine being the kind of person who would or could leave someone such a tip like that. I always give the woman with the stroller and the sign, "My Husband was

Deported," at least a dollar every time I see her. Although, I'll admit, sometimes I try not to see her. I once gave her a five and I heard a little girl behind me say to her mother, "How do we even know it's true?"

My Out 6 doesn't have to wonder if I'm telling the truth. He doesn't have to wonder if I'm really a server or where my husband is. I bet he doesn't even wonder what I'll do with that extra $69, or think, "I'm not giving that Ajumah any more money because she might spend it on fentanyl, whiskey, Doritos, or porn." Because I'm not just a homeless minority mother on welfare. I'm a server!

Besides, how does he even know if his own story is true? How can I know about mine? And does it matter? Isn't the act of sharing stories enough, regardless of accuracy? I mean, let's face it, as a species, truth isn't one of our strong points. Regardless of what one's sign says, we could all use a helping hand and some change.

The new manager stands over my shoulder. I hide my Franklin behind the others in my order book.

He asks, "Where'd your guy go? Didn't he need change?"

"Probably. I mean, don't we all?"

He squints at me, squeezing his thumb and forefinger together in front of the slit of an eye to indicate just how close I am to being written up. I offer him my open palms like I'm receiving alms, like I'm giving them. Then I kick open the swinging door.

Now, I am laden with the old man's old plates, five metal trays in my pocket with my money magneted onto them over their bill, and almost $3,000 in small bills splitting my plastic book bumping against my thigh. The weight of it pulls on my apron. But I keep going, dropping off checks regardless of whether my tables are still chewing, tightening my strings.

"Sorry. I need to lighten my load," I tell the chewers. "I might have to disappear for a little while. Take your time."

Some people get offended when I drop their checks mid-meal, as if I am abandoning them, just sticking them with the bill. Which is what I'm doing, essentially. Although, honestly, I've never abandoned anyone.

Curse of the Chinese Chicken Salad

12:31 PM

We're on lunch now, and today we have the special Asian salad that used to be called the Chinese Chicken Salad. Which is very curious, yes. I think it went from Oriental to Chinese, like going east to west. Or west to east, depending on how you're oriented. The old manager changed it to Asian, so as not to offend. But then she was fired. When did moving from specificity to generality become less offensive? I think this will offend the ghosts, the Southern Chinese ones that were burned out of their homes by the man this restaurant is named after. At least that's what I heard. At least there was a salad to honor them. At least it wasn't a milkshake. Then all the lids to our To-Gos would go missing again. A barista would quit again, or a busser, a dishwasher, or a cook. Or, God forbid, another server.

The employees are dropping like flies, but not cockroaches. That's only because the owner—the husband—comes in the wee hours to vacuum the ceiling—with his high-powered sucker—of defenseless, sleeping flies into the belly of his bag. Sometimes when I arrive in the early morning, I find him squatting in the server's station with a headlamp, wielding some unwieldy instrument like tongs in a box to snap roaches. He often leaves both items in the server's station beneath the counter, and I accidentally grab them when I'm searching for the red silicone square. I will examine this strange contraption and exclaim, *This isn't the mitt for the primo potatoes! This is for the roaches!*

I mean, why don't we just call it the tofu salad with peanuts? Or, the incredibly gaseous salad—leguminous, if that's a word. How come Oriental salads always have fried noodles in them? Perhaps it would be more accurate to call it the Californian Salad. Or, if they really wanted to hold onto this idea that this weird salad has roots in Asia, they could call it The Race We Tried to Exterminate in the Occident Salad. Or, the Gold Panner's Bitch's Salad. Or, the Miscegenation Salad because it's really just a combination of genetically modified hybrid greens tossed in rancid dressing and sold for $13—such an unlucky number, but not for the Chinese.

On Gravity

12:35 PM

The new manager doesn't like to cut because he's scared. He's afraid of too many people trying to get in the doorway to eat all at once, with too few of us trying to serve them too quickly, or not quick enough. But that's how we make our money. You got to cut. Then E can become A, D turns to B, C stays the same. Everyone gets more outside tables. The Backroom gets redistributed so that eventually, there is one last server standing and she, or he, or they, get the whole restaurant to themselves for at least a half an hour. That's what I get in the morning. It's almost like the day becomes a mirror of itself. You can't stop that. It's natural.

The new manager walks up behind me and taps me on my shoulder. He makes the edge of his hand into a blade and slides it across his neck, scrunching his cheek up to his left eye, making a duck sound.

"You are cut," he quacks, overly enthusiastically.

"Really? Really? It's barely even lunch," I say, incredulously. The end always comes as a surprise, even if you've been waiting for it forever.

"Re-stock. Then I'll check your sidework sheet."

Sidework sheets are a new thing. They hitchhiked in the new manager's briefcase on the first day he walked in, and I wish they would hitchhike on out.

Behind the back of the house and beside the dumpsters, pools of gray water are sprinkled with salt, chunked potatoes, with a fried egg on top—over easy, over medium, or over hard. I don't know. It's all looking pretty scrambled. The freezers are back here behind the behind of the back of the house. The walk-in is too which is colder than a witch's tit in a brass bra on the shady side of a mountain, as they say.

I have a list scribbled in my order book of the things that I need. *3 root beers, 5 Pepsis, 7 7-Ups, housing, Bloody Mary mix, diapers?* But I can barely read it in the dim light of the fridge. Metal shelves reach from floor to ceiling. Boxes are shoved in two-deep. I push my book into my apron, hike up my skirt and begin scaling the shelves that I know aren't bolted, clutching chunks of cardboard as I ascend to a place with no view.

My braids brush the ceiling of the walk-in. I spy the Bloody Mary mix at the very top. Do we even have to refrigerate it when it's unopened? I hold onto the shelf with one hand while I reach with the other, one leg stretched out into the air for balance, just dangling in the cooler. But the box isn't ripped down enough for me to get my hand in. I rest a foot on a milk crate for leverage, praying that I don't fall. Then I feel someone standing behind me. It's the busser, the Gumby one with the big afro, smiling. He takes his rubber go-go-gadget arm and reaches into the box, producing one unopened bottle of Bloody mix.

"Thanks," I say, jumping to the ground. "You're an angel."

He nods, smiling with his lips, bowing his head so that his afro dips, and exits.

Salvador emerges from an unlit corner, startling me, loaded with sour cream. He glares at me, then walks out of the walk-in belting out some Spanish song in a voice that makes my eyes turn instantly wet.

Behind the BOH, the prep cook stands over the dishwasher, squatting with his phone in hand. I go over to see what they're looking at. A meme of a woman in Daisy Dukes shaking her ass in circles, or figure eights, so fast, over and over.

"Wow," I say.

"Sí'" the dishwasher says, affirming my wonder.

I know it's just some computerized thing that makes her do it like that (or maybe not), but still. Wouldn't it be great if all we needed was one good skill and the world would just make a place for you? "You're the ass-shaker. Wonderful. Here's a home. You're the ass fucker. Amazing. Here's a room. You can sing a song that opens hearts. Stupendous. Have a car, no payments."

On top of a mat of flattened cardboard, the dull cook (not very sharp but rather ripped), lays on his back between puddles, with a jug of syrup in each hand. He presses them together like he's lifting weights.

"Chinita," he calls, putting down the Log Cabin. "Come." He pushes up his sleeves and readies himself to bench press me. "Come. Come." He pumps his eyebrows a few times, flexes his biceps. "Come on."

The whole back of the house, that is, those who are behind the back of the house on break, have lost interest in the meme now, as is the fate of all memes. They're all watching me, waiting to see if I'll let myself be a weight.

"Ay, cabrón," I say and run away, clutching too many cans to my chest, hoping that nothing will fall.

On Screen

12:35 PM

"Don't forget the salt!" the new manager says, scanning my incomplete sheet.

"But that was Ty's sidework yesterday and he didn't do it," I whine.

The manager points towards the ceiling at the haunted upstairs. "Salt," he growls.

I slip past a single dude sitting on the Tom Waits that blocks the door to the staircase. At least he has the presence to only take up a two-top.

"Sorry," I say.

"No worries, Love. Go ahead."

I prevent the door from re-latching by sticking a wad of napkins into it. If it closes, I'll be locked out and have to exit through the emergency exit door, circumnavigating the entire restaurant just to get to the front door. Like going to jail, directly to jail, without passing go and never collecting your $200 dollars, or whatever it is.

I scamper up the carpeted stairs where the servers sit at the end of a shift, thinking about quitting, until we count our tips. The cooks resent us for the inequity. "It's not us. It's the system," we say, walking fat.

A cool breeze blows through the dark hall. Someone must have left a window open. A sunbeam passes through the opaque curtain, illuminating dust motes floating like flaming fairies, flagrant before the dimming light.

"Now, what did I need?" I say, into that timeless space.

I turn the corner into the room that holds all the restocking supplies. With my little key attached to a ladle, I unlock the door to the room that contains all the alcohol, straws, salt, and POS tape. Why would someone want to steal POS tape for an antiquated printer? Or paper straws, for that matter—which we don't use anymore. We relapsed into plastic. But salt… I kind of understand salt.

There are packets of Splenda scattered across the floor that no one bothered to pick up. Probably Ty. I feel a warm breath on the back of my neck and turn quickly. Salvador stands too close behind me with one eyebrow cocked.

"What you doing up here?" he asks in a creepy voice.

"Why are you following me around this fucking restaurant?" I say, in the same creepy voice. "I'm restocking, asshole. What the hell are you doing?" I don't even know what the cooks restocking duties are. He points at a room I had no idea existed. "What? Showering? Jacking off? What?"

"No. Restocking too, dumb ass."

Then something catches our eye. At the end of the hall, the door to the room that holds all the monitors stands open. Colors dance through the diffused light of the hall, and for a second, I think it's spirits. I think it's ghosts and that we're all haunted. Salvador and I turn towards each other like teenagers in a B-rated flick about to make a bad decision, then walk in-step towards the room. If this were a real horror movie, we might be afraid. There might be scary music and we might be holding hands. And maybe we want to. But this is work, yo. We have our roles.

Our footsteps ring sonorously down the ancient hall. We silence our footfalls as we get closer to room 6. Or is it a 9? It's hard to tell which way the number leans, dangling like that one-by-one above the porch, still threatening to impale the next person who tries to Come Again. At least, last time I checked.

We enter the room and see the back of the head of a man with thinning hair, resting above a leather high-backed office chair, facing multiple screens. On one screen, Wile E. Coyote chases sheep as the sheep dog runs after. On another screen, Bugs Bunny chews on Betty Boop, inserting his carrot while other animated characters copulate all around. The chair swivels. It's the owner, the husband with his ice cream cone. He shoves the stump of it into his mouth, licking the side of his hand.

"You want to see something?" he says, still masticating.

Salvador and I look at each other, again, and both nod.

"Watch this."

He hits a button on his keyboard and his cartoons disappear. In a click, all six of his monitors light up. On various screens, I see myself in the morning, spilling coffee on the winemaker and taking down outside chairs; in the afternoon, bumping the busser; bitching at the baristas. On another, Salvador is hunched over the grill, turning, from time to time, to yell at everyone. And there's Ty clocking in late; the baristas dancing in their station. He zooms in on C-girl bent over. He pauses for a second before moving onto D-girl repeatedly washing her hands. Now I've entirely forgotten what I came up here for.

The owner makes the day move faster. The new manager waddles up and down the aisles like a penguin, until the owner finds what he's looking for. He presses rewind, and we watch the busser with the loaded dish bin trip on his own toe wearing a slight smile, dumping the contents of the dish bin onto the homophobe's suit. He rewinds and plays it again, and we all laugh like we couldn't laugh before. He rewinds it and plays it in fast-mo, or whatever it's called, and we laugh even harder, so hard that we are crying. He plays it in slow-mo. I think I see Rosanna push the busser, but I'm not sure. The owner rewinds it one more time and plays it at a more normal speed, freezing the frame on Ty's uncertain face looking devastated.

The End

1:00 PM

I stand in line behind Salvador, waiting for him to clock out. But he keeps typing his employee ID # erroneously.

"Will you fucking hurry up?" I say, in a rush out of principle. When really, I have nowhere to be.

He shoots me a look.

"Please?"

Finally. Bingo! He clocks out. Then I clock out and follow him down the narrow aisle through the kitchen. Outside, a shingle slides off the roof and breaks at our feet into pieces. We squint into the sky. There's the sun, peeking through, fucking finally.

Salvador hangs a right towards his brand new Tacoma to drive to Superburger for his next shift. See you tomorrow," he says, looking tired.

I hang a left towards my old car. "Hasta mañana," I say, feeling rich.

"Yeah, hasta mañana, Chinita. Enjoy the rest of your beautiful day. And those niños." He sighs.

"Yeah. You too. What's left of it." Already, I miss the morning.

I lean against the I-mark, still without rear shocks, trying to guess what's next, when a car pulls up, practically running me over, its music so loud and so strange. The passenger door flies open. My husband is at the wheel. He raises his eyebrows in lieu of a greeting and I hop in on the fly. The baby is asleep like a newborn in a car seat. The others listen, enrapt, to the ancient sounds of Gagaku written centuries ago by someone, somewhere on the peninsula now generally called Korea. The volume is turned up to the max. The children sit with their lips parted, eyes unfocused, seeing the unseen. I hope that they are breathing. I reel in my seat belt, an old stretched out thing that no longer retracts.

"How's it going?" I say in a hushed voice, putting my feet on the dash. I fold my apron into small triangles rolled upon triangles like a prayer flag: a three-sided compact green bundle folded in my fist, a shift completed, sticky and stained.

"Where to?" I ask.

"Dunno," he says, going straight towards the edge of the Pacific. Or, not "straight." Rather, "forward." It's a very windy road.

I toss my apron onto the dashboard. The strings unfurl. Then it occurs to me—I forgot to refill the salts! Oh no! But there's no going back until tomorrow.

Postscript

I'd like to say that our days became different, that we changed professions, bought a condo, a convertible, a Pomeranian. Although, thankfully, we did not. We moved back to the property where the intentional community once was. (It was simply subdivided. The mountainous, recreationally-zoned portion stayed with the owner's son and the rest of the property was sold to a group of overly ambitious entrepreneurs.) We hauled our canvas structures to the ridge, re-erected our tipi poles among the bottle caps, and resumed life as usual, whatever that means. My husband went to work in the vineyards, pruning lavender around grape vines and planting baby oaks. (Landowners get tax breaks on their vineyards if they replant some trees.) The children ate too much redwood sorrel and got the runs. They ran barefoot and got worms, and we parented, wondering how to survive in one of the wealthiest counties in the nation with a 0% vacancy rate.

We would do anything, we said, for our children.

But, how to live a beautiful life, do no harm, be compassionate, mindful while saving the world, the whales, the orangutans, money for college, the tread on our tires? *You look so tired, Hon. What's the matter? Don't you still want me?* It's so hard to get out of our down bags with the weight of the world compressing our chests like those x-ray blankets our friends in our sensory processing disorder group used to steal from the hospital. Yet, still, I rise happily to wait tables. But not Ty, I'm sad to say. He cooked his eggs. Inspired, I believe, by the concept of release.

It was pouring rain at his funeral. His mother's backyard looked like a scene from a mobster movie, sheltered by a canopy of black umbrellas—everyone beautiful, everyone glamorous, dressed in black with their makeup smeared, even the men.

On the other side of the crystal blue pool, beneath a pop-up tent, was a life-sized cardboard cut-out of Ty wearing a baseball cap backwards and a pair of wings. The boy had wings like that. There was a picture of him wearing them posted at his funeral too. I vowed, then and there, to never buy wings like that for my children. If they want them, they'll have to make their own.

At first, I thought the life-sized cutout of Ty was the barista with Lyme in real life, not cardboard life, because the barista sometimes wears his cap that way too. I think the barista was secretly in love with Ty. I mean, weren't we all? But the barista never showed. The manager never showed. I was the only one there from the restaurant, as everyone else had to work. It just happened to be my day off.

Ty's stepfather was trying to plant this strawberry bush in a hole over the bundle of ashes that was once Ty (or was him still). But the bush wouldn't fit, so he dug deeper, saying, "This plant is sort of like my Ty. Needs a lot of attention, always makes a mess, and could be too big for his britches."

Everybody laughed, not knowing all that Ty could carry, and all that he could not.

Sometimes I think Ty has gone to cardboard heaven. Sometimes I think I still see him on billboards—on a hair product ad in Rite Aid, or as a reincarnated Ralph Lauren model by the railroad, smoking a Salem Light. But those are just illusions, other models still living.

In the mornings, at the restaurant, while staring out the little round window of the front swinging door, I sometimes think I see Ty across the street in his black hoodie, next to his car. He lights a cigarette with the cook's stove-lighter. The long plastic stick shoots a blue butane flame and I do not go out to extinguish it. Ty dons his wings and I do not go out to hold him down. He stretches them and flaps, knocking branches from the trees. They clatter across the parking lot. He picks one up, snaps it, and is gone.

Acknowledgements

It took worlds to write this book and to all those worlds I am most grateful. First, I wish to thank the forests that sustained and housed us through the writing, thank you to the creeks and the fields. I am beyond grateful to Black Lawrence Press, Diane Goettel, Abayomi Animashaun, and the Black Lawrence Immigrant Writing Series, the Friends of Writers, Sustainable Arts Foundation, Elizabeth George Foundation, the Vermont Arts Council and National Endowment for the Arts. Thank you. Lan Samantha Chang and Justin Torres for your encouragement, and Deb Allbery for everything. T. Geronimo Johnson and Laura van den Berg for their initial words regarding this project. Boz, Karen Brennan, Vanessa Hua, Sarah Cypher, my cohort and all my writing groups from all times, going way back: Minh-ha Pham, Patricia Wakida, Liz Madans, Claire Light, Liz Henry, Charlie Jane Anders, Melanie Hilario, Susan Ito, Rice Papers, LexiCats, Annalee Newitz, Maggie Tokua-Hall, Makenna Goodman, Shingai Kagunda, Alexander Chee, Hannah Silverstein, Liz Ross, Rashda ("Sonny") Buttar, Annette Wong, to name a few…I wish to thank all the landlords and employers, my parents, and pets. Green Valley Village, The Wild Nest. Howard's. Thank you. And first, and foremost, to all of my family, known and unknown, human and non-human, everywhere.

Sasha Hom lives off-grid in a yurt on a 600-acre land co-op amid 5,800 acres of conserved land situated within Vermont, an odd-shaped state (but aren't they all?) upon a very large continent amid oceans. She has four children, many goats, fowl, and a dog. In addition to homeschooling her children and herding small ruminants, she runs a refuge/laboratory for arts and ecologically-oriented folx, and works on the farms of others. She was a Holden Minority Scholar at Warren Wilson College where she earned her MFA, a recipient of a Sustainable Arts Foundation grant, a Brink Hybrid Literary Award, and Elizabeth George Foundation grant. Her work can be found in *Exposition Review, Brink, The Leon Literary Review, The Millions, Literary Mama, Kweli Journal, Viz. Inter-Arts, Journal of Korean Adoption Studies,* and anthologies.